CRASH COURSE

Joe grabbed the edges of the floating surfboard and tried to lie on top of it, his legs dangling off the end. But the back of the board sank under his weight, and the front angled up out of the water. Then the whole thing shot out from under him, flew into the air, and splashed down a few feet away.

Jade grinned and said, "Paddling is simple—staying on the board is the tricky part. Let me show you how."

As she started to wade toward the surfboard, Joe noticed a large wave rolling in. He realized it was going to break almost on top of him, and he started to duck and cover his head with his arms.

But as he did, he saw something else—a runaway surfboard tumbling through the rushing water, crashing straight down at Jade!

Books in THE HARDY BOYS CASEFILES® Series

Available from ARCHWAY Paperbacks

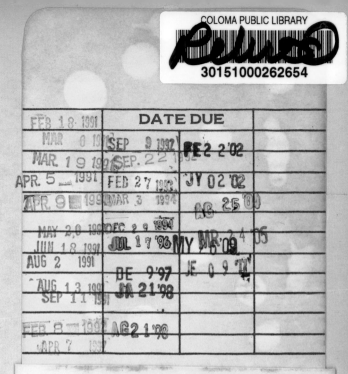

This book is a work of fiction. Names, characters, places and incidents are either the product of the author's imagination or are used fictitiously. Any resemblance to actual events or locales or persons, living or dead, is entirely coincidental.

AN ARCHWAY PAPERBACK *Original*

An Archway Paperback published by
POCKET BOOKS, a division of Simon & Schuster Inc.
1230 Avenue of the Americas, New York, NY 10020

ISBN: 0-671-67488-9

First Archway Paperback printing June 1990

10 9 8 7 6 5 4 3 2 1

Printed in the U.S.A.

IL 7 +

FRIGHT WAVE

Chapter

1

"WHAT WAS THAT?" Joe Hardy blurted out. Something had jolted him awake. He looked around quickly and saw his brother, Frank, sitting in the seat next to him.

"Just a little turbulence," Frank said. "Go back to sleep."

Joe started to do just that, but a second later he was sitting bolt upright, his blue eyes showing no sign of drowsiness. He remembered where they were headed. They had flown a long way from their hometown of Bayport, and now Joe was eager for a first glimpse of their destination.

Joe ran a hand through his blond hair and started to lean across Frank for a glimpse out the window. A sharp tug at his waist reminded him that he was still strapped into his seat.

"Whoa!" Frank exclaimed. "There's not much to see. From up here everything still looks pretty small." Just then Frank felt his ears pop as the plane dropped through the sparse cloud cover. He knew they'd soon be on the ground.

The wing outside Frank's window dipped down as the jet went into a tight turn, and the bright morning sun streamed into the cabin and directly into Frank's brown eyes. The bright light made his brown hair look lighter than it really was. He squinted and pulled down the shade.

"Please make sure your seat belts are securely fastened," a female voice crackled over the intercom, "and return your seats to the full upright position."

"Why?" Joe asked nobody in particular. "What difference does it make what position my seat is in?"

"Well, it might make a big difference to me," a voice from behind them answered. It was the voice of their father, Fenton Hardy. "The back of your seat's been in my lap for about two thousand miles—and my legs have been asleep for the last five hundred. How about giving an old guy a break?"

Joe shifted his muscular, six-foot frame. The movement made him realize that his whole body was stiff, and there was a dull pain in his neck and shoulders that he vainly tried to rub away. "Airplane seats are definitely *not* designed for comfort," he mumbled.

"Not if your flight is over thirty minutes long or you're over five feet tall," Frank added.

There was a soft bump as the wheels hit the runway, and a loud roar as the pilot threw the huge jet thrusters into reverse. They all strained forward in their seats as the three-story-tall jumbo jet rapidly slowed from 200 MPH to taxi speed.

When the plane finally came to a complete halt and the seat belt sign winked off, Frank and Joe jumped out of their seats. They were at the door before the flight attendant had a chance to pick up the intercom microphone and say, "Aloha—and welcome to Hawaii!"

It took almost an hour to claim their luggage, pick up their rental car, and drive to their hotel. "It took only eight hours to go five thousand miles," Joe commented as his father unlocked the door to their hotel room, "but it took sixty minutes to go the last ten miles."

Fenton Hardy fumbled with the key, and Joe rolled his eyes at his brother. They were both loaded down with luggage, most of which belonged to their father. The older you are, the more stuff you have to drag around, Joe thought.

Finally the key turned and the door swung open. Frank and Joe staggered into the room and dropped the bags in the middle of the floor. Joe let out a low whistle as he looked around. "You didn't say your client was *rich*, Dad."

They were standing in the middle of a large

living room furnished with a leather couch, several expensive-looking upholstered chairs, and an antique writing desk. On two of the sides of the room was a door leading into a bedroom and private bathroom. They turned slowly, taking it all in.

Joe looked over at his father. "Who is your mystery client, anyway?"

"You could say it's a large nationwide company," Fenton replied vaguely. "And just remember—it's *my* client. You're here on vacation. The only thing you have to do is sit on the beach, enjoy the scenery, and stay out of my hair."

Frank walked out on the balcony overlooking the Pacific Ocean. He looked down twenty-five floors to the waves lapping the shore of the world-famous Waikiki Beach.

Joe joined him and said, "What are we waiting for? It's time to hit the beach!"

"Right," Frank replied. "Let me just get out of these clothes and into my suit." He grabbed his suitcase and headed for a bedroom. "What about you?" he asked over his shoulder. "Don't you want to change first?"

"I'm one step ahead of you," Joe said, flashing a grin as he started to take off his pants.

Frank stifled a laugh when he saw what his brother was wearing under his clothes. "You're not seriously considering actually wearing those *outside,* are you?" he asked.

Joe glanced down at his bright, baggy Hawaiian

flower-print swim trunks and said, "You're just jealous because you don't have a pair."

A few minutes later Frank and Joe were on the beach, walking along the shore, letting the warm saltwater wash over their bare feet. High-rise buildings crowded right up to the edge of the long, thin stretch of sand known as Waikiki, on the Hawaiian island of Oahu.

"I was reading a guidebook on the plane," Frank said, scanning the skyline. "This beach is less than a mile long—"

"Lighten up!" Joe chided him. "We didn't come to Hawaii to study. We came to have fun in the sun!" He bent down, scooped up a handful of water, and splashed the back of Frank's head.

Frank whirled to face him, and a movement behind his brother caught his eye. "Yeah," he said, nodding toward the ocean. "Maybe we could even learn to surf really well."

Joe turned and watched a couple of obvious beginners floundering in the shallow water. Their rented surfboards were stenciled with the name of a nearby hotel. Then beyond them—out in the serious waves—he saw something else. A lone surfer, racing down a cresting wave, then swiveling around and swerving back up the rushing wall of water.

The board was almost vertical to the water as the front end edged over the lip of the breaking

5

wave. Then the surfer pivoted again, and the board flew out of the water, sending a spray back over the top of the wave. Joe thought the ride was going to end with the board and rider spinning off in different directions—but the surfer turned the board in midair, slammed back down into the water, and rode the dying wave all the way to shore.

Joe could hardly believe what he had just seen. As the surfer carried the board out of the water, he got an even bigger shock.

Frank noticed the look on his brother's face. "What's wrong?" he asked.

Joe kept staring and whispered, "It's a girl!"

She put down the surfboard and moved toward the Hardys, as if she had felt Joe's intense stare. Her hair was straight and black, glistening with saltwater. She looked faintly Asian, with brilliant green eyes. Even in her surfing bodysuit— a short-sleeved wet suit that covered her from her neck down to her knees—Joe thought she was beautiful.

"Aloha!" she called, smiling at Joe as she walked closer. "Do I know you from somewhere? I mean, the way you were looking—"

"No!" Joe blurted out. "I just . . . um . . . that is—"

"He just forgot that it's impolite to stare," Frank interrupted. "I'm Frank Hardy, and this is my brother, Joe."

"My name's Kris Roberts," she replied. "But all my friends call me Jade because—"

"Because of your eyes." Joe finished her sentence.

She looked at him more closely, a puzzled expression on her face. "That's right. How did you know?"

Joe shrugged. "Just a lucky guess." He wanted to say something else, but no words came.

There was a brief, awkward silence.

"Well, it was nice meeting you," Jade finally said. "Maybe I'll see you around," she added, looking right at Joe.

Then she was gone, walking down the beach toward a small group of surfers. All at once she stopped, turned back, and called out, "Hey! I don't suppose either of you malihinis knows how to surf, do you?"

"Mali-what?" Joe managed to get out.

Jade laughed. "Malihini. A newcomer, a visitor. I've lived here most of my life, and some islanders still call me a malihini."

"Really?" Joe responded, glad that his voice had finally returned. "You could have fooled me. I thought you were Hawaiian."

"With a name like Roberts? Not likely. My father still has relatives in Ireland, and my mother was Japanese. Almost everybody in Hawaii has come from somewhere else. There aren't too many native Hawaiians left.

"You didn't answer my question," she continued. "Do you know how to surf?"

"Not really," Joe admitted. "But I'll give it a try. How about you, Frank?" he asked.

7

"No thanks," Frank said. "I'll just sit here on the beach and admire your technique."

"Then I don't have to scrounge up another board," Jade replied. "We can use mine. Come on!"

The two of them waded out until the water was about waist-deep. It was fairly calm, with just a slow, rhythmic swell. Most of the big waves were breaking farther out. Every once in a while one did crash down around them, though, throwing Joe off balance.

Jade held the surfboard steady in the water. "The very first thing you need to do," she explained, "is play with the board."

"*Play* with it?" Joe asked doubtfully.

"That's right. Roll it around. Flip it over. Lean on it. Get the feel of it."

"Okay," Joe said. He took the board and flipped it over. It had three slight ridges running the length of the board, which ended in three sharp fins at the back. The front of the board tapered to a narrow point. He pushed one end underwater and felt the pressure as it popped back to the surface.

"That's good," Jade said just as Joe was concluding that surfing was a very boring sport. "Now it's time to learn how to paddle."

"That sounds easy enough," Joe remarked. "I bet you start by lying down on the thing, right?" He grabbed the edges of the floating board and tried to lie on top of it, his legs dangling off the end. But the back of the board sank under his weight, and the front angled up out of the water. Then the whole thing shot out from under him, flew into the air, and splashed down a few feet away.

Jade grinned and said, "Paddling *is* simple—staying on the board is the tricky part. Let me show you how."

As she started to wade toward the surfboard, Joe noticed a large wave rolling in. He realized it was going to break almost on top of him, and he started to duck and cover his head with his arms.

But as he did, he saw something else—a runaway surfboard tumbling through the rushing water, crashing straight down at Jade!

The roar of the surf made it impossible to shout a warning. There wasn't time to think, only time to react. Joe lunged through the water, desperate to reach Jade before the wild surfboard did. His arms strained forward, and he just managed to grab her shoulder with the tips of his fingers. He dug in and jerked her backward.

Jade barely got out a startled "Hey!" before Joe pushed her head under water, shielding her with his body.

Then the wave and the fiberglass missile slammed home, and Joe Hardy's world went black.

Chapter
2

FRANK WAS IN THE WATER in a flash, splashing through the foamy remains of the deadly wave. He had watched helplessly as the surfboard landed on his brother. He reached Joe's limp form as Jade came spluttering to the surface, gasping for air.

Frank grabbed Joe under his arms, lifting his head and shoulders out of the water. Jade quickly took one of Joe's arms, and together they started to haul him out of the water. Before they reached the shore, two other surfers joined them and helped carry Joe.

They laid him down gently in the sand. Joe was breathing, but that was his only sign of life.

Frank knelt down next to him and looked at the bruise on the side of his brother's head. It was too early to tell how bad it was.

"Ugh," Joe mumbled in a minute, squinting against the bright sunlight. "What a horrible dream."

Frank smiled with relief. "Yeah? Why don't you tell me about it?"

Joe struggled to a sitting position, propping himself up with one hand and rubbing his forehead with the other. "I dreamed I was on the beach in Hawaii. But every time I met a beautiful girl, my brother would come barging in and wake me up."

He glanced around, and his eyes found Jade. "This dream seems okay," he said softly, starting to grin but stopping almost immediately to wince in pain. "Except for the extra-strength aspirin commercial booming in my skull," he added.

"What happened out there?" someone asked.

Frank noticed that a small crowd had gathered around them. "That's what I'd like to know," he replied. He stood up, pushed through a couple of people, cupped his hands over his eyes, and scanned the shoreline.

He spotted the surfboard, lying half in the water and half on the wet sand. It seemed harmless enough now. But a few minutes earlier it had been inches away from doing very serious damage.

Frank waited a minute to see if anyone would claim the abandoned surfboard.

Joe got up slowly—a little wobbly, but otherwise all right—and joined his brother. "I don't know about you," he grumbled, "but I think I'll go over and kick the stupid thing a couple of times. It'll think twice before it tangles with me again."

Frank looked at him. "Doesn't it seem kind of strange that whoever owns that surfboard just left it there?" he suggested.

"Not really," came the reply, but it wasn't Joe's voice.

Frank turned to see a big Hawaiian guy standing off to one side. His black hair hung in wet curls over his forehead. Joe figured he must be at least six foot five and probably tipped the scales at around two-fifty. Frank recognized him as one of the surfers who had helped carry Joe out of the water.

Frank studied him carefully. "Why do you say that?"

"Crazy haoles don't know the first thing about surfing," the big guy said, and snorted. "They rent some cheap board like that from a hotel, and then they think they can go out and get vertical or shoot inside the tube the first time out. Some of them even think the wax goes on the *bottom* of the board."

"Hay-oh-lees?" Joe repeated slowly. "Could you translate that?"

"Anybody who's not Hawaiian," Jade explained, joining them. "It usually means a tourist from the mainland. But sometimes he calls me that when he thinks I'm cutting into his lane on a good wave.

"This is Al Kealoha," she continued. "Al's one of the few full-blooded Hawaiians you're ever likely to meet. So be nice to him. He really belongs here. The rest of us are just visitors. Al helped me pick out my first surfboard, and he taught me everything I know."

Al grinned broadly. "That's a good line—I think I'll use it after you take the Banzai. Then I'll start my own surf camp. Girls will come all the way from the mainland begging me to make them the next Jade Roberts. Yeah, I like it."

"The Banzai?" Frank asked. "What's that?"

"The Banzai Pipeline," Al replied. "It's one of the biggest surfing events of the year. Didn't Jade tell you? She's a top contender in the women's division."

Joe turned to Jade. "I knew you were good, but—"

"It's really not that big a deal," she insisted. Joe thought she looked a little embarrassed. "There are lots of girls who are just as good as I am—better, even."

Al gave a low chuckle. "I can think of only one who even comes close."

Frank didn't hear Al's last comment. His mind was on something else. "Is there any prize money in this competition?" he suddenly asked.

"Sure," Jade nodded. "A few thousand dollars. No big deal. Why?"

"Oh, no reason," Frank replied casually. "Just wondering. That's all." He happened to glance over at Joe and saw how pale his brother was. "I think one surfing lesson a day is just about all you can survive. You need to rest."

Joe rubbed his forehead again. "I don't need rest, but I think you're right about the surfing for the day. What else is there to do in Hawaii?"

"Have you been up to Nuuanu Pali yet?" Jade asked. "You haven't seen Oahu if you haven't been to Nuuanu."

"Well, in that case, we'd better get going!" Joe insisted.

A few minutes later Jade and the Hardys were sitting in an old army surplus, camouflage green jeep. Jade was driving, and Joe sat next to her. Frank had to share the backseat with a surf-board. The sun beat down on their heads. If the jeep had ever had a convertible top, it was long gone.

"What do you do if it rains?" Frank asked.

Jade shrugged. "I get wet."

The wind whipped through her hair as they rumbled down the road, and Joe realized he was staring at her.

He tried to think of something to say—again. He frowned slightly and cleared his throat. "There's something I need to know," he began.

Her green eyes sparkled. "Just ask," she responded.

"If this is Oahu—where's Hawaii?"

"Hawaii is the name of the state—and the biggest island in the chain," Jade explained. "But most of the population lives here on Oahu."

Joe noticed that they were headed inland, toward the lush, green mountains that shot up behind the city of Honolulu and hemmed it in. "You know," he said, "I have no idea where we are or where we're going. How about you, Frank?"

"Haven't a clue," Frank admitted.

"We're on the Pali Highway," Jade said. "It goes over the Koolau Mountains to Kailua on the other side of the island."

"You seem to know the island pretty well," Frank observed. "Have you lived here all your life?"

"Just about," she replied. "My father and I moved here when I was only two."

"Just the two of you?" Frank prodded.

Joe saw a troubled look pass over Jade's face. He put his hand on her shoulder. "Don't pay any attention to him," he told her. "He collects information like other guys collect comic books. He'll keep asking questions as long as you keep answering."

"It's all right," Jade replied. "I don't mind talking about it. We moved here from California right after my mother died." She paused for a moment. "I'm not sure how she died, and I don't know why we ended up in Hawaii.

15

"Not that I'm complaining," she continued, her smile slowly returning. "Not too many folks get to grow up in paradise!"

They had been moving steadily higher into the mountains. Jade pulled off onto an access road that didn't go very far before it dead-ended in a small parking lot.

"End of the line!" Jade shouted, bringing the jeep to an abrupt stop and jumping out.

Frank and Joe were right behind her. Frank stopped to look around. To the east and west rose the Koolaus, completely covered in a carpet of green growth. To the north and south blue ocean could be seen beyond the green.

Frank turned to say something to Joe but saw that his brother had followed Jade to a concrete platform. It was very out of place right there and more than a little ugly. Something obviously seemed to be holding their interest, and Frank jogged over to see what had captured their attention.

As he came up next to Joe, he said, "So what's the big—" He stopped in midsentence, sucked in his breath, and whispered, "Oh."

They were standing at the edge of a cliff that plunged almost a thousand feet straight down. The sheer side of the cliff was completely covered in green. Frank strained to make out the bottom.

"This is Nuuanu Pali," Jade said loudly. She had to raise her voice because of the wind gusting around them. "*Pali* is the Hawaiian word for 'cliff.' We're standing above the Nuuanu valley. Down there"—she gestured—"is Honolulu. And over there"—she pointed in the opposite direction—"is Kailua, on the other side of the island."

"Nice view," Joe shouted over the roar of the wind. "Maybe we should come back on a nice, calm day, though."

Jade laughed. "The trade winds rip through here from the Kailua side almost constantly, trying to find a way through the mountains."

"I think I can see Waikiki Beach," Frank ventured, "and the hotel where we're staying."

"Yeah, and this wind is probably strong enough to carry you all the way back there," Joe observed. "If you get a good running jump and then flap your arms real hard . . ."

Frank took another long look down the steep cliff. "You go first," he suggested.

"I've got a better idea," Jade said. "Let's *drive* back in my car. We can stop downtown and get something to eat. You may still be on mainland time, but around here it's lunchtime— and I'm starving."

Jade took them to a sidewalk lunch stand in downtown Honolulu. Joe thought it looked a lot like any other American city, except almost everybody wore Hawaiian shirts—and instead of hamburgers, fast food meant noodles in a Styrofoam cup with a plastic thing that wasn't quite a fork but wasn't exactly a spoon either.

17

They sat at a table near the curb and watched the cars buzz by while they ate. Finally Joe asked the question that had been following them around ever since they'd left the beach. "Do you really think that close call with the surfboard was an accident?"

"What do you mean?" Jade asked. "What else could it have been?"

"Maybe somebody doesn't want you to surf anymore," Frank suggested.

"Yeah." Jade nodded. "My father. But I don't think he'd throw a surfboard at me. What are you guys getting at?"

"Well, there is the prize money," Joe reminded her.

Jade shook her head. "I told you already. It's not a big deal. A few thousand dollars, that's all. Besides, the surfers around here are a pretty tight-knit group. We're like family. None of them would ever do anything to hurt me."

"Okay," Frank said. "So maybe it isn't anybody you know. But it could be—"

Frank didn't finish his sentence because that was when he heard a screech of tires. He watched mesmerized as a car swerved off the road, jumped the curb, and smashed into an empty table twenty feet from them.

It didn't stop there, though. It kept plowing ahead. And Joe and Jade were right in its path!

Chapter
3

"LOOK OUT!" Frank shouted, leaping from his chair at the same time. He would be in the clear, but what about his brother and the girl? Their backs were to the car. Joe, seated on the other side of the table, couldn't see the vehicle bulldozing a lane toward him.

Frank grabbed the table with both hands and pushed it as hard as he could—right into his brother.

Joe caught sight of the onrushing car when the edge of the table slammed into his stomach. He let out a startled *"Oof!"* as he toppled over backward. Instinctively, he grabbed Jade, yanking her out of her seat. She landed on top of him, knocking the wind out of him, but he managed to wrap his arms around her and roll away from the path of destruction.

The next moment the wooden table was reduced to kindling and splinters, and a streak of blue metal and black rubber flashed by, inches from Joe's face.

The blue sedan didn't even slow down as it swerved back onto the road. Frank's heart was pounding, and the blood was rushing through his body at a furious rate. Without even thinking, he picked up a toppled chair and flung it at the car.

The flying chair smashed into the sedan's rear window and then rebounded, bouncing off the trunk and clattering to the pavement. The car kept moving—but Frank could see a spiderweb of cracks spreading across the shatterproof glass from the point of impact.

Frank watched as the blue sedan weaved frantically through the traffic and disappeared around a corner.

The people at the other tables were buzzing with excitement and concern. Frank heard someone behind him say, "What happened?" as another voice added, "Are you all right?"

It took a moment for Frank to realize they weren't talking to him. It was Joe and Jade they were asking about.

Joe was already on his feet, pulling Jade off the ground. "You know," she said, "my life was pretty normal until you guys showed up. Maybe you're bad luck or something."

"It's beginning to look that way," Joe agreed, brushing dust and splinters from his clothes.

"I don't think luck has much to do with it," Frank replied grimly.

"What do you mean?" Jade asked.

"I mean I might buy two accidents in one day," Frank said. "But this wasn't an accident. That guy was aiming at us. He never even tried to slow down."

"You don't know that for sure," Jade countered.

"No, we don't," Joe said. "But we will—once we find the driver of that car."

"What do you mean you didn't get the license number?" Joe demanded as they headed back to the hotel in Jade's jeep. "You're the one who's supposed to think of those things, remember?"

"I was kind of busy," Frank snapped. "Remember?"

"Oh, well," Joe said. "It's a small island. How many blue sedans can there be?"

"Lots," Jade said softly, as she pulled up to the front entrance. "There are almost a million people in Honolulu, and most of them have cars.

"But nobody I know owns a car like that one," she added, "and I know almost all the surfers in the islands. So let's just drop the jealous surfer theory, okay?"

The jeep rolled to a stop, and Frank climbed out the back. "Not jealous," he pointed out, "just greedy. Besides, it could have been a rented car—like the surfboard."

Joe started to get out, too. Then he turned to look at Jade. "Will I see you again?" he asked, trying to sound casual.

A smile passed over her lips. "Maybe," she murmured. "Now get out of here. My dad will start to worry if I don't get home soon."

That night Joe dreamed he was surfing with a beautiful woman. At first she was a stranger, then she turned into Jade. They were having a great time until a blue sedan—with cheap, rented surfboards lashed to its wheels—came rolling across the waves, its horn blaring angrily.

There was something wrong with the horn, though. It made a kind of ringing noise instead of honking. Joe thought it sounded just like a telephone. Slowly he realized that it *was* the telephone, and the dream slipped away as he drifted back to the waking world, groping for the receiver.

"H'lo," he mumbled into the phone. "Whozit?"

"It's Jade," the voice on the other end whispered hurriedly.

Suddenly Joe was wide awake. "Jade! What is it? Where are you? What's wrong?"

"I'm down in the lobby, but we've got to get out of here fast!"

Joe was already reaching for a pair of jeans with his free hand. He cradled the receiver between his ear and shoulder and used both hands to wrestle his pants on. "We're on our way!" he exclaimed. "Hang on!"

He dropped the phone and shook his brother awake. "Come on, Frank!" he shouted. "Jade's downstairs—and she's in trouble!"

"Wha—" Frank replied drowsily. "What's the problem?"

Joe threw some clothes in his brother's face and raced out the door. "I'm going to get the elevator," he called back. "I'll hold it for thirty seconds, and then I'm out of here!"

"I'm right behind you," Frank assured him, swinging his legs out of the bed and onto the floor. He pulled on a pair of shorts, grabbed the shirt Joe had tossed at him, and slipped his feet into his beat-up deck shoes. Then he was out the door. A second later, he was back, snatching up the shoes Joe had forgotten to put on.

Frank hit the hallway running, just in time to see the elevator doors start to slide shut. He put on a burst of speed, shoved his arm between the closing doors, and pried them open.

"Come on, come on!" Joe urged once both boys were on the elevator. He jabbed the button marked *L* over and over again.

Frank reached out and gently grabbed his brother's wrist. "Take it easy," he said. "Nothing's going to happen to her in the hotel lobby."

"Right." Joe nodded, relaxing a bit. When the elevator doors opened on the ground floor, he bolted out.

23

"It took you long enough!" Jade said, grabbing his hand and pulling him toward the door. "We've got to get going before it's too late."

They hurried out into the morning sunlight and climbed into the waiting jeep. Jade turned the key and the ancient engine coughed to life. Frank hopped into the backseat, which was occupied now by two surfboards. "Too late for what?" he asked, wedging himself in. "What time is it?"

"Oh, about eight-thirty, I guess," Jade responded. Her mood seemed to lift once they were on the road.

"You didn't answer my first question," Frank persisted.

"Yeah," Joe agreed. "What's up? Where are we going?"

Jade kept her eyes on the road and said, "We're going to Waimea, on the north shore of the island. That's where you get the really big waves this time of year."

Joe studied her carefully, his brain still a little sluggish from sleep. "You mean you rousted us out of bed because—"

Jade glanced at him and flashed a big smile. "That's right. Surf's up!"

If it had been any place other than Hawaii—and anyone other than Jade—Joe probably would have been furious. But the ride was beautiful, and so was she.

By the time they got to Waimea Bay, it looked

to Joe as if it were shaping up to be another great day in paradise.

Even though it was still early, there were already a lot of people on the beach. Jade found a place to park the jeep and hopped out. "Wait here," she said, "I've got to change. I'll be right back."

Frank and Joe got out, stretched, and took in the sights. Jade had been right about the surf—*up* was definitely the word for it. Some of the waves rose fifteen feet or more before curling over and crashing back down.

There were surfers everywhere, on the beach and in the water. Most of them wore the same kind of one-piece, short-sleeved wet suit that Jade had worn the day before. But Joe noticed the suits came in almost every possible color combination.

The suit that Jade came back wearing was subdued by the standards of Waimea. It was almost solid black, with a band of emerald green stripes running down each side. Joe thought she looked stunning, but he kept his cool. "Nice outfit," he said. "It matches your eyes and your car."

She gave him a curious look. Then she glanced over at the old jeep with its faded camouflage paint job and smiled. "I guess I just like green."

"Good thing, too," Frank commented. "Because this whole island is green."

Jade pulled one of the surfboards out of the

back of the jeep. "Come on," she said, tucking the board under her arm, "let's hit the beach."

Joe took one step out onto the sand and quickly backpedaled, yelling, "Yow! That's hot!"

Jade looked down at his bare feet. "You get used to it after a while. But maybe you should put on your shoes," she suggested. "I'll meet you down by the water."

Frank waited while Joe got his shoes. He watched the surfers slashing down the towering blue cliffs in the deep water. He didn't think there were any tourists or amateurs taking on those waves. Out there, you had to know what you were doing, or you wouldn't be doing it for very long. Or anything else for that matter, Frank thought.

Joe strolled up, wearing his battered high-tops. "Where's Jade?" he asked, his eyes making a quick search of the beach. "Oh, there she is."

He took off at a jog, coming up behind the girl and grabbing her arm. She turned to face him— but it wasn't Jade. Same height, same build, same hair, even the same suit, but most definitely not Jade.

Like Jade, she had oriental features. Hers were more Chinese than Japanese, though—and she didn't have Jade's piercing green eyes.

"Oops," he whispered. "Uh, sorry. I thought you were someone else."

She gave him the once-over, smiled, and said, "I'm sorry, too. But if you don't find whoever you thought I was, let me know. Maybe we can work something out.''

''Well, I see you've already met Connie,'' a voice called out. It was Jade.

''Connie Lo, meet Joe Hardy,'' she said.

Connie grinned. ''Wiped out by Jade Roberts again. This trophy's already yours, I take it.''

Jade laughed. ''You've already got a boyfriend, Connie. Besides, Joe doesn't really surf.''

Connie frowned slightly, and her voice took on a serious tone. ''I'm beginning to think that might be a real plus at this point.''

Then she noticed what Jade was wearing and her grin was back. ''Hey, cool suit, kiddo,'' she quipped, lifting her arms to reveal identical green stripes. ''You've got great taste. And since I already have your suit,'' she continued, ''how about letting me try out that new board of yours?''

''You've got it,'' Jade replied, holding out the surfboard for her. ''What's mine is yours—any time. You know that.''

''Thanks,'' Connie said. ''I'll try not to get it wet.'' Then she turned to Joe. ''You be good to her,'' she warned him, ''or I'll break your legs.''

Frank walked up in time to hear the last remark, before Connie sprinted off into the raging surf. ''What was that all about?'' he asked.

''Oh, that's just Connie's way,'' Jade said. ''She's like a big sister. We surf together all the time. She's one of the best. Check her out.''

Frank and Joe saw Connie as a black-suited

figure on a gleaming surfboard, starting to slide over the edge of a huge, breaking wave. Suddenly there was a muffled *pop pop!*

The board bucked violently, and the surfer started to pitch sideways into the raging surf, arms flung wide. The relentless wall of water slammed into the small dark figure and engulfed it.

Chapter

4

FRANK WHIRLED IN THE DIRECTION that the noise had come from. High on a cliff he saw another dark-clad figure. This one wasn't holding a surfboard—it was holding a high-powered rifle.

Frank squinted, tried to bring the figure into better focus, but it was too far away. He couldn't make out any details. He turned to tell his brother what he had seen, but Joe was gone.

Frank caught sight of him diving into the rough water and swimming toward something floating loose in the swells. It was Jade's new surfboard, the one Connie had been riding. Frank knew his brother was a strong swimmer, but he was wearing long pants. By now they would be totally soaked and very heavy.

Frank wouldn't have hesitated to follow his

brother even if he hadn't been wearing shorts. The fact that he was made him feel a little better as he kicked off his deck shoes and splashed into the rolling water. Not much, but a little.

He started to close the gap, stroking through the water strongly and evenly.

Joe had managed to power his way to the drifting board first. The nose was sticking out of the surf at a sharp angle, and the back was buried beneath the blue water as if it were tied to an anchor. Joe knew that the anchor must be Connie, dangling unconscious from the ankle tether that a lot of the surfers used so they wouldn't have to chase their boards after a wipeout.

He dove beneath the surface and easily spotted Connie's limp form swaying upside down in the deep current. A few strong kicks took him the short distance. He wrapped his arms around her chest and strained to turn her around and haul her up to the surface. But it felt as if there were lead weights on his feet, dragging him down. Then he remembered his jeans. They might as well be lead weights, he realized.

Joe started to wriggle out of his water-logged pants, and as soon as he let go of Connie, something pulled her up to the surface like a fish being reeled in. Joe followed her up and found his brother struggling to get Connie onto the surfboard.

"The next time someone tells you to keep

your pants on," Frank said, "don't listen to them."

Together they flopped the unconscious girl onto the board. Frank didn't know how much water she had taken in, but he knew they had to wait until they got back to shore to find out. The waves crashing around them were tremendous. He clambered onto the wobbly board, knelt over her, and paddled quickly to shore.

On dry land he pressed his palms firmly into her back. A small trickle of water dribbled out of her mouth, and then her body was wracked by a torrent of wet coughs.

Her eyes fluttered open. "Awesome wave," she groaned. "But I didn't see the shark coming."

"Shark?" Frank repeated.

Joe nodded to the front of the board, near where Connie's head still rested. "The one with the big teeth," he said.

Frank looked down and saw what his brother was talking about—two neat holes drilled clean through the fiberglass.

A crowd had gathered around them now, and Frank slipped away from them, motioning Joe to follow. "You know those bullets were meant for Jade," Frank stated flatly when they were alone.

Joe glanced back to see Jade kneeling next to her friend. "Same hair, same build, same suit, same surfboard," he noted grimly. "Yeah, I know. So let's find whoever fired the slugs and break his arms. I'd break his spine, but he probably doesn't have one."

"Good idea," another voice chimed in. "I'll help." It was Al Kealoha, the massive Hawaiian surfer.

Seeing Al reminded Joe of something. "Just the guy I wanted to see," he began, before his brother could say anything. "I think you said something the other day about only one other surfer being almost as good as Jade. I was just wondering who she is."

Al jerked his head back toward the small crowd. "You just hauled her out of the Pacific."

"You mean Connie?" Frank asked.

The surfer nodded. "Connie's got all the right moves. She can still beat just about anybody in the women's circuit."

"Anybody but Jade," Joe added.

"You're real *akamai* for a malihini," the Hawaiian said.

"A smart tourist," Frank translated.

Joe glanced at his brother. "Since when do you speak Hawaiian?"

Frank shrugged. "There's a lot of useful stuff in those guidebooks."

"Well, do the guidebooks say where to find suspects after you discover that your number-one choice is the victim's best friend and almost ended up as another victim?" Joe muttered under his breath.

Al shook his head slowly. "You guys are wasting your time if you think a surfer's behind this. We stick together. We don't stick knives in our friends' backs."

As Al started to walk away from the Hardys, a guy with shoulder-length blond hair stopped him by clutching his arm. He had the tan and muscular build of a surfer, but he wasn't dressed for the water. He was wearing a T-shirt and baggy shorts.

"Hey, Al. Wait up," Frank heard him say. "I just got here, and I heard that something happened to Jade. Is she all right?"

The big Hawaiian gripped the newcomer's shoulders. "Hang steady, Nick," he said calmly. "It wasn't Jade—it was Connie."

Frank saw the look of concern on Nick's face change to one of horror. "Connie," he croaked. "No . . . it couldn't be . . . I mean, I thought . . . Where is she? I've got to see her!" He broke away and pushed through the crowd.

There was a brief commotion, and then the Hardys saw him hustling Connie out of the circle of onlookers, his arm around her shoulder.

Frank and Joe looked at each other. "Are you thinking what I'm thinking?" Joe asked.

"I'm thinking we should find out more about this Nick character," Frank answered.

It took a while for the police to arrive on the scene. By the time they finished interviewing everyone and filling out their endless forms, it was late in the afternoon.

Joe could see that Jade was pretty badly shaken. It was finally starting to sink in that someone wanted her in the past tense, and Joe knew how hard that was to handle. So he decided to wait until she had calmed down a little before bringing up the subject of someone trying to eliminate her again.

Finally when they were in her jeep, driving back to Honolulu, he decided the time was right. "So who's Nick?" he asked casually.

"Nick?" Jade spoke distantly. Her mind was somewhere else—either on the road or replaying the events of the last two days. "Oh, Nick Hawk, Connie's boyfriend. Why?"

"His reaction seemed a little . . . strange," Frank suggested.

"Well, someone just took a couple of potshots at his girlfriend," Jade snapped. "How is he supposed to react? How am *I* supposed to react?"

"Hey, we're just trying to help," he assured her. "If you say the guy's all right, we'll just drop it. Okay?"

She nodded. They drove without speaking for a few minutes. Jade finally broke the silence and said, "Nick's a little edgy. He used to be a pretty hot surfer. But he shattered his knee a couple of years ago in a real serious wipeout.

"He can walk okay now," she continued. "He can even surf a little. But his competition days are over. So he channels all his energy into Connie's surfing. He's more like her trainer now than her boyfriend. I think winning means a lot more to him than it does to her."

"How badly do you think he wants Connie to win?" Frank prodded.

Jade shook her head. "Not enough to kill me. We may not all like each other, but we're still part of the same big family."

"Surfers are really important to you, aren't they?" Joe observed.

"Is your brother important to you?" she replied, not waiting for a reply. "Other than my dad, they're all I've got."

"You told us about your mother," Frank said. "But don't you have any other relatives?"

Jade shrugged. "None that I know of. I don't even know how my mom died. My dad doesn't like to talk about it. I think her death must have been very painful for him. I think we moved to the islands because he wanted to cut off the past."

A brief smile passed over her lips. "Sometimes I feel like we didn't exist before we came to Hawaii."

The sun was getting low in the sky by the time they got back to the hotel. Jade turned off the ignition and the engine shuddered and died. She shifted in her seat so she could take in both brothers. The tension on her face was evident, and Joe wanted to do something to make it disappear.

"Look," she began, "I'm sorry I yelled at you before. But this is all just a little too weird, you know? Who'd want to kill me? And why?"

"We'll find out," Joe promised. "But maybe

you'd be safer staying with us instead of going home. Our dad used to be a cop, and he still has some powerful connections."

Jade reached out and took his hand. "Thanks, Joe. But I really should go home. Besides, even if Nick Hawk is behind this—and I'm sure he isn't—I don't think he'd try anything at my house. I'll be all right."

"At least give us your address and phone number, in case we have to reach you," Frank urged.

She took a piece of paper out of the glove compartment, scribbled something on it, folded it once, and placed it in Joe's palm. Then she closed his fingers over it. "Keep it in a safe place," she said. "Our phone number is unlisted, and my father doesn't like my friends to come to the house. Not many people know where we live."

Reluctantly they let her go and watched as she pulled the jeep out into traffic.

Frank's eye was caught by a blue sedan pulling away from the curb just then. It moved in right behind the old green jeep. At first he thought the rear window of the car was frosted. No, he decided, that wasn't right.

With a jolt, he recognized the spiderweb pattern of cracks, snaking out from where the chair he had thrown had smashed into the glass.

Chapter
5

"THAT'S THE CAR," Frank said, grabbing hold of his brother's arm.

"What?" Joe said.

"That's the car," Frank repeated. "The car from yesterday. Look at the rear window. That's where I hit it."

"And now it's following Jade," Joe cried out. "We've got to stop him!"

"We need a car," Frank said.

He jogged over to a man in a red coat who was standing next to a sign that announced Valet Parking. "Can I borrow your jacket for five minutes?" he asked.

The man eyed him warily. "How do I know you'll bring it back?"

Frank waved Joe over, turned back to the

parking attendant, and said, "I'll leave my brother as collateral. Okay?"

The man took one look at Joe's wide frame moving toward him and stripped off the jacket. "Here," he said, handing it to Frank. "Keep it as long as you want. No sweat."

Frank darted into the parking garage, thrusting his arms through the sleeves of the attendant's red jacket as he ran.

He slowed down as he neared a door next to a large window that looked into the garage. Through the glass, Frank could see rows of car keys hanging on hooks on the wall. He also saw a fat, bald man leaning back in a chair, his feet propped up against a desk.

Frank tugged on the sleeves of the red jacket. They were a little short, but they would do. He walked through the door. "The guy in twenty-five-fifteen wants his car," he announced.

The bald head turned slowly. "Yeah? Where's his ticket?"

Frank smiled. "He lost it. But he says he'll pay the lost-ticket charge." Frank stuck his hand in his pocket and pulled out a key attached to a small metal tag with a number engraved on it. "He gave me his room key to prove it was his car."

"You carhops come and go so fast, I don't even know your names. I don't think I've seen your face around before." Finally the fat man grunted and tossed something at Frank. "It's in stall thirty-eight. If anybody asks, you took it while I was in the john.''

Frank snatched the key ring out of the air and headed for the door.

Joe was keeping the nervous parking attendant busy. His muscular build could make him look threatening even if he was smiling, and sometimes that worked exactly to his advantage. Behind his smile Joe was wondering what his brother was up to.

About two minutes later a white, four-door sedan cruised up next to him. The driver rolled down the window and tossed something out. Joe ducked, and it sailed past him. It hit the attendant square in the chest. It was his red jacket.

Frank poked his head out the driver's-side window. "Let's put this baby in gear and get out of here," he said.

Joe ran around to the other side and slid into the front seat next to his brother. The car was already moving as he slammed the door shut.

"I hope Dad wasn't planning on going out tonight," Frank said. "This is the car we rented at the airport."

At the end of the driveway, Frank turned in the direction the jeep had gone a few minutes earlier. "There should be a map in there," he said, nodding toward the glove compartment. "See if you can find the street Jade lives on."

Joe found the map, unfolded it, and spread it

out in his lap. His eyes scanned it carefully, comparing street names to the one Jade had written down. It was slow going. All the Hawaiian names looked the same to him—mostly vowels with a few consonants thrown in here and there. "Got it!" he finally announced.

He glanced out the window, spotted a street sign, and then looked at the map again. "Turn right at the next intersection," he directed his brother.

Frank flicked the turn signal and moved over into the right lane. In the rearview mirror he could see a black van behind them do the same. Frank turned the corner, and the van followed.

He didn't say anything about it to Joe. He wasn't sure yet, and he needed his brother to navigate without any distractions.

Joe looked up from the map and peered out the window. They passed a few more streets. "Whoa!" he suddenly yelled. "Back up! I think we were supposed to take that street back there."

Frank made sure there was no traffic in the oncoming lane, cranked the wheel hard to the left, and came around in a tight U-turn. The black van held its course, moving off in the other direction. Frank let out a small sigh of relief, but then he noticed that their unwanted shadow was pulling into a driveway. Maybe he lives there, he told himself, but the van backed out into the road. Pretty soon it was close behind them again.

They rolled up to a stoplight. "This is it," Joe said. "Turn right here."

Frank didn't move. He checked the rearview mirror. The van was still there. He checked the traffic on the cross street. There were a few cars in the distance, but the intersection was clear for now.

"Come on," Joe urged. "You can turn right on a red light. It's legal."

Frank flicked on the turn signal, but he kept his foot on the brake. He glanced left and right. Cars from both directions were almost at the intersection. A few more seconds ticked by.

Joe reached out and shook his brother's shoulder. "Frank? What's wrong? Why are we just sitting—"

Frank slammed his foot down on the gas pedal, and the tires screamed. The car shot straight ahead. Horns on both sides blared a frantic warning. Frank ignored them, his hands gripping the wheel, his foot jamming the gas pedal into the floor.

They flashed across the intersection just before the cross traffic closed the gap.

"—here?" Joe finished his sentence on the other side.

Frank relaxed. He took his foot off the accelerator, and the car slowed down.

"What was *that* all about?" Joe demanded.

"We had company," Frank explained. "But I think we lost them."

There was a screech of rubber somewhere behind them. Joe snapped his head around to get a look out the back window. "Was it a black van? Sort of like ours back home?"

Frank's eyes darted to the rearview mirror and saw it, tires smoking and the back end fishtailing as the van imitated his stunt.

"Hang on," he muttered through clenched teeth. Then he punched the gas again, trying to put some distance between them and the black van. At the first street he came to he turned left, then right a block later, and another left at the next street.

Frank kept his eyes locked on the road in front of him, but still he had to know. "Is it still there?"

"Yeah," Joe said. "But we're pulling away. He probably can't corner too well in that thing. A few more sharp turns should do it."

A steep hill loomed in front of them. The road didn't go up it or around it—it went through it. "Turn where?" Frank shouted as they entered the tunnel.

On the other side, the road ended abruptly. They were surrounded by a towering wall of rock splattered with brownish green plants and vines. On a small sign were the words Diamond Head Park.

Joe searched for another exit. "There's got to be another way out of here," he insisted.

Frank slammed on the brakes, and the car skidded to a halt. "Yeah," he replied, "over the top. This is Diamond Head—an extinct volcano. We're sitting at the bottom of the crater."

They could hear the van coming through the tunnel, the rumble of the engine echoing off the walls. "I guess it's too late to go back the way we came," Joe said.

They got out of the car and looked up the side of the ancient volcano. The sun was beginning to set, and deep shadows filled the crater. Frank could just make out a lazy zigzag pattern near the top, and his eyes traced its downward path. "There's a trail over there," he said, pointing off to the left.

Behind them, they heard a car door open, then another. Joe whirled around and saw the black van. There were two unfriendly-looking men standing next to it. One of them was wearing a gray suit. A ragged scar slashed down the left side of his forehead.

The other one was wearing a windbreaker over his shirt. Joe knew that guys who wear coats on hot days are usually hiding something inside them.

"We want to have a little talk with you," the man in the suit called out.

"So start talking," Joe said as he backed around the rented car. He wanted to put a nice, thick steel barrier between himself and the concealed "conversation piece" he was sure the man's hand was resting on under the coat.

"What now?" he whispered to his brother.

"Don't worry," Frank said in a low voice. "I've got a plan."

"Great. What is it?"

"Run," he said. Then he turned and bolted toward the trail.

Joe was right on his heels. "I was afraid that was the plan!" he shouted in Frank's ear. He glanced back and saw the two men lumbering after them. Frank and Joe had a good head start, and they were in better shape than their pursuers. They could easily stay out of firing range—as long as they had someplace to run.

Joe wasn't worried about himself. He was thinking about Jade. If they didn't find a way out of the crater soon, they might not be able to stop the driver of the blue sedan—if it wasn't already too late.

"What do we do when we get to the top?" Joe huffed.

Frank looked up. He figured the volcano was about seven hundred feet high, but it would take a while to reach the top on the switchback trail. "I haven't figured that out yet."

"Terrific," Joe muttered.

They jogged past a dark opening in the side of the volcanic wall. It looked like a cave. But Frank thought it might be something else. He doubled back and peered inside. It was pitch black.

His brother joined him, poking his head into the gloom. "Great place to get trapped," Joe said.

"Not if this is what I think it is," Frank said, stepping inside. "Come on. This could be our ticket out of here."

Joe shrugged and followed him. They moved slowly through the darkness, stumbling over invisible debris. Frank felt his way around a corner and found himself in a chamber filled with long shadows and an eerie orange glow.

"What is this place?" Joe asked.

Frank pointed at the source of the light. It was the last rays of sunlight streaming in through a long, narrow opening carved into the far end of the volcanic wall.

"It's an old gun emplacement from World War Two. They turned Diamond Head into a kind of armored fortress. After the war they pulled out all the hardware but left the holes. The crater is honeycombed with these old pillboxes."

"So you were hoping maybe we'd find some old guns, too?" Joe asked.

"No," Frank said. "I was hoping we could lose those guys in the maze of tunnels. But it looks like this is a dead end."

Joe wiped the sweat off his forehead. "Well, maybe if we double back before—"

"Hey, Pete!" a muffled voice shouted from just outside the tunnel. "I thought I heard something over here in this cave. Maybe we should check it out."

"Yeah," came the reply. "Let's get it over with."

Chapter

6

JOE SCANNED THE CHAMBER for any kind of weapon. A rock, a brick, anything to give them a fighting chance. A shadow high up on the wall cast by the setting sun caught his eye. He looked up and saw a rusty metal rod hanging from the cement ceiling.

Frank saw it, too. "Steel-reinforced concrete," he whispered. "This place was built to take a lot of shelling."

Joe jumped up and grabbed the rod. It sagged under his weight and then snapped off. Joe dropped softly to the floor, holding a four-foot chunk of solid steel.

Frank saw another metal bar suspended above the narrow entrance to the room. He didn't think it would break off so easily—but he had an idea.

He leapt up and grasped it with both hands. He swung his legs up and planted his feet on the wall above the doorway. Then he pulled himself up until his head was touching the ceiling. Anyone walking into the room wouldn't be able to see him unless he looked straight up.

Joe knew what his brother had in mind. He flattened himself against the wall next to the entrance and held the steel rod ready to swing.

They could hear footsteps in the dark corridor, scuffling toward them. A figure appeared in the doorway, and Frank pounced. His full weight came down on the man's shoulders, toppling them both to the floor.

Joe didn't budge. He didn't want to reveal himself. He was waiting for the second man. Seconds ticked by. Nobody came through the passage. Joe glanced from the doorway to the two figures rolling and grappling on the dusty floor. First Frank was on top. Now he was on the bottom—and the man above him was raising a rock over his head, about to bring it down in a crushing blow.

Joe moved out in the open and swung the steel bar. The blow connected with the man's forearm. He screamed in pain and clutched at his arm with his other hand.

"Hold it right there!" a voice boomed from the darkness.

Joe lifted the metal rod and spun around. The man in the dark gray suit stepped into the dim chamber.

Joe could see the scar more clearly now. It cut through the man's eyebrow and continued on down his cheek. Whatever had made the mark had barely missed his left eye. Then Joe noticed that he was holding something in his hand.

Joe could see it wasn't a gun. It was a badge.

"FBI," the man said. "Assaulting a federal officer is a serious offense. I think you two have some explaining to do."

Frank got up off the floor and helped the injured man to his feet. "Who are you guys?" he asked. "Why are you following us?"

The man holding the badge turned to him. *"I'll* ask the questions. You'll give the answers. Clear?"

"That depends on the questions," Frank said.

"Okay, try this one. What happened to Fenton Hardy?"

"Something happened to Dad?" Joe blurted out.

"Fenton Hardy is your father?" The agent's eyes narrowed as he turned to his partner, who was still holding his bruised arm. "Next time get all the facts first. We've just blown half a day."

He looked back at the Hardys. "Sorry about all this. Come on, let's get out of here, and I'll explain."

As they walked down the trail the FBI agent talked. "I can't tell you very much. I don't know a whole lot myself. We're just watchdogs. Your father is working on a sensitive case for the

Bureau, and my partner and I are supposed to make sure nothing happens to him.''

Frank nodded. ''I see. You knew the car was rented to him. So you followed it, thinking he was in it. Then when we tried to give you the slip, you figured something must be wrong—like maybe we kidnapped him or something.''

''Say, you'd make a pretty good detective yourself,'' the man said. ''You've got all the answers.''

''Not all the answers,'' Frank said coolly. ''I still don't know who you are.''

The agent smiled thinly. ''Well, I see we're at the end of the trail, and there's your car. Drive safely now. We wouldn't want you to get hurt, would we?''

Joe didn't notice the icy exchange between his brother and the man in the suit. He was worried about Jade, and he wanted to get moving. ''Give me the keys,'' he insisted. ''I'm driving.''

Frank didn't respond. He was studying the two FBI agents. He watched them walk back to the black van, get in, and drive away. Then he turned to his brother. ''I think we'd better go back to the hotel and talk to Dad before we do anything else.''

''Not before we check on Jade,'' Joe demanded.

''Our little detour took almost an hour,'' Frank replied. ''If nothing happened to her while we were running around in here, she's probably safe—for now.''

''At least let me call her,'' Joe persisted.

"It will only take a couple of minutes to get back to the hotel," Frank pointed out. "You can call her from there."

Fenton Hardy was waiting for his sons when they walked through the door of the luxury suite. He glanced at his watch. "I was starting to get worried," he began.

Joe braced himself for a lecture—something about responsibility, letting your parents know where you are, and not taking the car without permission. "Before you say anything," he cut in, "I can explain . . ."

His words trailed off when he saw the people sitting on the couch behind his father.

Fenton Hardy glanced back over his shoulder. "Yes." He nodded. "I'm sure you could, but I've already heard most of it. I'd like you to meet Kevin Roberts," he continued. "I think you already know the young lady sitting next to him."

Jade smiled at Joe. He thought she looked more exotic than ever.

"My daughter tells me some strange things have been happening since she met you," Kevin Roberts said.

"I spotted a car following me home today," Jade explained. "I think I shook him off, but it really spooked me. I told my father everything, and we decided to talk it out with you. I'm really sorry to drag you into this."

"You didn't drag us into anything," Frank assured her.

"That's right," Joe said. "We jumped in with both feet."

"I still don't understand why anyone would be after me," Jade said.

Frank exchanged a quick glance with his father and Joe. "I think I may have come up with something. There may not be much prize money in surfing, but what about illegal gambling? What if somebody has bet a bundle on another surfer in the Banzai?"

"It's a possibility," Fenton Hardy said. "There is organized crime in Hawaii, but not on the same scale as on the mainland."

Kevin Roberts nodded. "The big crime families from the mainland haven't been too successful in breaking the local mob," he said. "At least, that's what I've read in the papers," he added.

"Well, we all agree that there seems to be a definite threat to Jade's life," Fenton concluded. "What surprises me, Mr. Roberts, is why you came here instead of calling the police as soon as you found out."

Jade's father looked uncomfortable.

"We're talking about your daughter's life!" Joe snapped when Roberts didn't answer.

"I know," Kevin Roberts replied slowly. "That's why I think we shouldn't say anything to the police."

Joe was confused.

"If organized crime is behind this, there may be crooked cops on their payroll. I came to the same conclusion as Frank about heavy gambling involvement."

"So what do we do now?" Jade asked.

"You stay here tonight," Fenton replied. "Frank and Joe will sleep in one room, and you and your father can use the other."

Joe looked at his father. "What about you?"

"I have a hunch that I won't be getting much sleep," Fenton said. "I've got a lot of arrangements to make for you for tomorrow."

"While you're up," Frank said, "have one of your FBI friends run a check on a surfer named Nick Hawk."

At dawn Fenton Hardy hustled his sons and Jade onto an interisland commuter plane.

"Where are we going?" Joe asked.

"Maui," his father replied. "It's an island about ninety miles southeast of here. It's a little bigger than Oahu, but it's a lot less crowded."

"What do we do when we get there?" Jade wanted to know.

"Stay away from crowds," Fenton said. "There'll be a rental car waiting for you at the airport. Keep moving around until we can find out who's after you—and why."

He turned to his older son and handed him a slip of paper. "Frank, here's a number where I can be reached if I'm not at the hotel. Try to check in a couple times every day."

Just as Fenton Hardy had said, a car was waiting at the airport. Frank called his dad to let him know what their plans were. Joe got behind the wheel, and a few minutes later they were driving along a twisting, two-lane road. Jade was sitting next to him, and Frank directly behind him, looking out the window. On the left was a steep hillside, covered with tropical plants. On the right the ground fell away sharply, and the Pacific waited several hundred feet below.

"Jade should be safe," Frank said, "as long as we keep on the move."

"Well, we're moving right along," Joe observed, keeping his eyes on the curvy road ahead. "Although I'm not sure where we'll end up."

"This road follows the coastline south to the town of Hana," Jade explained. "But how long do we keep driving around?"

Frank shrugged. "A few days, maybe—maybe less."

"Do you really think your father can help?" Jade asked.

"With access to the FBI computers and the description of the blue sedan with the broken rear window," Joe said, "you'd be surprised what he might turn up."

Frank pounded the seat with his fist. "I knew I forgot something!"

"Your Bermuda shorts?" Joe ventured.

"No. I forgot to tell Dad about those two FBI agents."

"So what? We're all on the same side, aren't we?"

"I hope so," Frank muttered almost to himself.

Joe gestured out the window. "Relax. We're in paradise, remember? If that guy behind us would just stop tailgating, I could slow down and enjoy the view myself."

Then there was a loud, metallic *crump*, and the car lurched forward suddenly.

"Hey!" Joe yelled. "That guy just rear-ended us!"

There was another *crump*, and they surged forward once more.

"He did it again!" Joe shouted, struggling to keep the car on the road.

Frank spun around and got a good look at the other vehicle. It was a pickup truck, and this time he made sure to get the license plate number. But he didn't think it would do much good. The truck was larger and heavier than their car, and he guessed the driver wouldn't stop ramming them until he pushed them over the edge of the cliff.

Chapter

7

INSTINCTIVELY JOE SLAMMED ON the brakes, but when he did, the truck just rammed them harder. They skidded closer to the cliff edge. Then he switched tactics and hit the gas pedal.

But there were too many twists and turns in the road. He would barely pull away before he'd have to slow down for another curve. And then the pickup was right on top of them. *Crump!* The bumpers of the two vehicles smacked together.

"Is there any place up ahead where we can get off this road?" he shouted. *Crump!* His head snapped back and bounced off the headrest.

Jade shook her head. "How did they find us so fast?"

"I don't know! But I'm not going to stop and ask!"

Crump! Joe knew that sooner or later one of those blows would be more than he could handle, and the car would tumble over the side and plummet into the ocean below. Up ahead, the road climbed sharply, but it was a pretty straight shot, and Joe figured it was the only one he'd get.

"Hang on!" he screamed, and punched the gas pedal to the floor.

The car pulled away from the pickup and sped up the road. At the top of the rise, there was a sharp bend to the right, but Joe didn't plan on making the turn. He yanked his foot off the accelerator and smashed it down on the brake. At the same time, he cranked the steering wheel all the way to the left.

The front tires screeched and smoked. The rear end swung out to the right, and the car spun around in the middle of the road. It skidded backward a few feet and softly bumped into the guardrail on the outer edge of the curve.

Then Joe was jamming the gas again, and the car squealed back down the road. The pickup truck was plowing up the hill, hugging the inside lane, away from the cliff. Joe stayed on the same side and aimed straight for the truck, his foot glued to the gas pedal.

He was grinning wildly. "Up for a little game of chicken?"

Now they were close enough to see the terrified expression on the truck driver's and passenger's faces. He tried to pull off the road, but the shoulder was too narrow. The tires on the left side hit the steep incline and rolled up it. The whole truck tilted crazily to one side. Joe swerved back into the outer lane and zipped past just as the pickup rolled and fell over.

Frank twisted around to see the wreckage. "We've got to go back and get them out of there," he said.

"Are you crazy?" Joe burst out. "They were trying to kill us!"

"Frank's right," Jade said. "We can't just leave them there."

Reluctantly, Joe stopped the car, put it in reverse, and started to back up. He could see someone trying to climb out of the pickup truck. Then there was a sharp *crack,* and the rear window of their car shattered.

Frank dove for the floor. Joe ducked, pushing Jade's head down with his right hand at the same time. "I don't think they want our help," he said.

Frank was staring at a brand-new hole in the window over his head. "I think you're right," he replied. "Let's get out of here."

Joe slammed the gearshift lever and pressed down hard on the gas pedal. The car shot forward, and they left the overturned truck far behind.

They didn't stop until they came to a gas station with a pay phone. Frank hopped out and ran over to the phone. He punched in the number his father had given him.

After a few rings, a female voice came on the line. "Federal Bureau of Investigation, Honolulu office."

A few minutes later Frank hung up the phone and walked back to the car.

"Any news?" Joe asked.

"Well, there's good news and bad news," Frank said. "Which do you want first?"

"Let's start with the good," Joe suggested.

"Okay. The good news is those goons in the pickup truck were probably the last we'll run into."

"Did they find the owner of the blue sedan?" Jade asked.

"No," Frank said, turning to her. "But they didn't have to. That's where the bad news comes in. It looks like your friend Nick Hawk owes money to almost every bookie in town—and he's been putting down some heavy bets on Connie Lo to win the Banzai Pipeline. They arrested him about an hour ago."

"I can't believe it," Jade said. "Did he confess?"

"No," Frank admitted. "But the evidence is pretty strong. He was in deep. If he couldn't pay off his gambling debts soon, he was going to be shark bait. With you out of the way, Connie would be the top contender."

Joe looked at Jade. He could see that she was

fighting back tears. He reached out and touched her. Her arm felt stiff, and her fist was clenched tightly at her side. "I'm sure Connie didn't know anything about it," he said. "It's over. Try to put it behind you. You can go home now."

Jade looked at him. "I don't think I want to go back yet. I need some time to clear my head."

Joe smiled. "Hey, no problem. It's a sunny day, and we've got a full tank of gas. What do people do for fun on Maui?"

"I don't know," Jade said, perking up a little. "Play golf or hang out at the beach, I guess."

"Hmm, tough choice," Joe said, scratching his chin.

"Not really," Frank remarked. "We didn't bring any golf clubs."

"So that leaves the beach," Joe said.

"Okay," Jade nodded. "Just as long as we steer clear of surfboards. I don't even want to think about surfing today."

"No problem," Joe said, starting the engine and putting the car in gear.

"Yeah," Frank agreed. "Because we didn't bring any swimsuits either."

It was past noon by the time they rolled into Lahaina, a small town perched on the western coast of the island. A hundred years earlier it had been a major seaport for the islands, and it still had the look of an old-fashioned sailing port. Weathered clapboard buildings hung out over the bay, suspended a few feet above the water-line by sturdy wooden beams.

Frank noticed that instead of seedy dockside bars and musty tackle shops, the port was now home to expensive boutiques and custom T-shirt stores. Outside one of the stores, Frank spotted a public phone.

"Pull over for a minute," he said. "I'd better let Dad know where we are."

After he made the call, they drove along the coast. Beyond the small town on the bay, the beach took over again. Swimmers, surfers, and strollers dotted the shoreline.

"Just stop wherever it looks good," Jade said. "All the beaches in Hawaii are public."

Joe saw something floating in the air over the water. "Is that a guy in a parachute?"

Jade looked where he was pointing. "He's para-sailing. See that motorboat out there? The parachute is attached to the boat by a long line. It's the closest thing to a roller coaster you'll see in Hawaii. I've heard it's a lot of fun, but I've never tried it."

Joe steered the car onto the sandy shoulder. "Well, let's find out."

Frank studied the billowing, rainbow-colored shape being towed across the sky. "I think I'll sit this one out. Parachutes are great if you're in a burning airplane. I don't feel like putting one on when I'm already on the ground. You two go ahead and try if you want."

Joe and Jade walked across the sand to the water. They watched the motorboat make a wide turn, slowing down as it headed toward the beach. As its speed dropped, the parachute in the air behind it glided down. The boat turned again. Now it was barely coasting, just a few feet from the shoreline. The parachute swung over the beach as it dipped down, and the man strapped into it landed lightly on his feet.

Joe could see two men in the boat. They both looked like native Hawaiians—dark skin and thick black hair. The skipper was standing, holding the wheel with his left hand. He worked the throttle with his right hand, easing it back slowly. Without throwing out an anchor, it was tricky to hold the boat steady in one place. It looked like he had had a lot of practice at it, though.

The other man jumped overboard into the waist-deep water and waded ashore. He gathered up the flapping parachute and helped the rider out of the harness.

Joe grabbed Jade's hand. "Come on, here's your chance."

"*My* chance?" she said. "What about you? This was your idea!"

"Ladies first," Joe insisted. "Besides, you were the one who said it was fun."

The smiling Hawaiian from the boat held out the parachute harness. "You want to give it a try? Only ten bucks."

Joe shook his head. "Two for fifteen," he haggled. "First her, then me."

The man's grin widened. "Okay. You hold the chute while I get her strapped in."

Joe wrapped his arms around the bundle of multicolored nylon, making sure not to tangle the lines leading to the harness. Jade stepped into the harness and put her arms through the shoulder straps. The Hawaiian checked the straps that crisscrossed her hips and chest, making sure they were all snug and secure. He patted her on the back and flashed another big grin.

"All set," he called to Joe. "Just wait until I'm back in the boat, and then let go." He ran into the water and splashed his way back to the motorboat.

Jade tugged at the harness. "I'm not sure this is such a hot idea."

"It's too late now," Joe replied. "I already paid him—and I don't think I could get you out of that thing, anyway."

Joe saw the Hawaiian climb back in the boat, and he got ready to let go of the parachute. But then he saw another boat pull up next to it. This one was a flat, sleek white speedboat. Painted on the side was a red lightning bolt. On the stern, Joe could see the name *Big Deal*.

Two men were on the speedboat. They shouted something across to the other boat. Joe couldn't make out the words, but he could see that the newcomers were backing up their argument with a pistol. Then the long, thick line that ran between the boat and the parachute was untied and tossed over to the more powerful speedboat.

Jade glanced nervously at him. "Joe? What's going on?"

Joe dropped the parachute and ran toward her. He heard the deep growl of the diesel engine as it roared away. He saw the slack go out of the line. The parachute billowed and rose upward.

Just as Jade was jerked off her feet and into the air, Joe leapt up and grabbed the harness. The parachute dipped slightly from the extra weight. Joe's feet brushed the sand.

"Let go!" Jade screamed. "You'll be killed!"

Joe clutched tighter. He didn't know what he was going to do, but he knew Jade was in danger and needed his help. Suddenly there was no ground beneath his feet. The parachute started to gain altitude rapidly.

After catching his breath, Joe looked down. The Pacific Ocean sparkled far below him already. How high had they soared? Fifty feet? A hundred? It was impossible to tell. Either way, it was too late to change his mind now.

He'd never survive the fall.

Chapter

8

THE SPEEDBOAT SKIMMED OVER the water, towing the parachute far from the shoreline. Joe's arms were starting to tire—the harness cut into his skin and burned the palms of his hands. He didn't know how long he could hold on, and he didn't want to find out the hard way.

"What do we do now?" Jade yelled.

With the wind rushing through his ears and the speedboat engine blaring below, Joe could barely hear her. "There's a Swiss army knife in my right front pocket," he shouted. "See if you can get it."

She reached around and managed to pull the knife out of his pocket. "Okay, I've got it. What next?"

"Cut the line!"

Jade opened the three-inch blade and stared at it. "It's going to take a while."

"I know," Joe responded. "But it's all we've got—unless you have a better idea."

Jade shook her head and started sawing at the thick nylon line. Joe twisted his head around and looked back at the island of Maui. He had his doubts that they could swim that far—and he had even bigger doubts that whoever was in the speedboat would give them a chance to find out.

He scanned the area for nearby ships. In the distance, he thought he saw a few navy battleships. They were too far away to take notice of a lone parachute, though.

The speedboat was headed in the direction of a small island. Maybe, if they got a little push from the wind, they could make it there. If they came down on dry land, Joe thought they might stand a chance of getting out of this alive.

They could run. They could hide. They could make weapons out of sticks and rocks. It wasn't much, but it was better than floundering in the water, waiting to get picked off.

"Got it!" Jade suddenly yelled.

The feeling of being dragged through the air abruptly fell away—along with the rope that splashed down into the blue water below.

The parachute started to drift downward, but the stiff trade winds were much stronger out in the open water, giving them a little extra lift and pushing them right where Joe wanted to go.

The speedboat circled underneath, like a hungry shark, waiting to see where the parachute would come down.

Frank had seen the speedboat pull up next to the Hawaiians' boat, but he was too far away to see what was going on. He didn't know anything was wrong until he saw Joe lunge at the parachute harness just as it lifted Jade into the air.

He ran down to the water, but the boat was already far out to sea. He watched the brightly colored parachute grow smaller in the distance. Just like that, Joe was gone as the rumble of the big diesel engine faded away. All Frank could hear then was the high-pitched whine of jet-skis, droning along the shoreline.

The two Hawaiians in the small motorboat watched in silence as the speedboat raced away. Frank waded out into the ocean, waving frantically to get their attention, but they didn't notice.

Frank swam out to the boat, grabbed hold of the gunwale, and hauled himself out of the water.

That got their attention. "What do you think you're doing?" the man clutching the wheel asked sharply, twisting to face him.

The other man moved toward Frank, fists clenched. "Crazy haoles. First you steal our parasail ride. Now you think you can steal our boat, too?"

Frank held out his hands. Both men were stocky and muscular. Although Frank was taller than they were, he doubted that he had a weight advantage over either of them. Even if he could take them out, he didn't want to start a fight.

"You've got it all wrong, guys," Frank quickly said. "When they stole your parachute, they kidnapped my brother and a friend of ours. So crank up the engine and let's get going."

"Go where?" the skipper replied. His anger had subsided, and now he looked at Frank with mild curiosity. "You can't take a boat like this into the interisland channel. It's too rough out there."

"Yeah," the other man agreed. "Besides, what would we do even if we *could* catch up with them? They had guns, man. *Big* guns."

"You can't just sit here and do nothing!" Frank yelled. "How about the coast guard—or the navy?"

"Good luck," the skipper said. "By the time you get to a phone and cut through all the red tape, that boat will be long gone."

"Terrific," Frank muttered.

He spun around to dive back in the water and saw something lashed to the side of the boat. He had climbed in from the other side, so he hadn't noticed it before. It looked like a cross between a motorcycle and a snowmobile—except it didn't have any wheels or treads.

Frank turned back to the two Hawaiians. He pulled a soggy wallet out of his soaking wet pants. "How much do you want for the jet-ski?" he asked.

"You'll never make it on that thing," the skipper said. "We just have it in case the engine breaks down and we have to ferry people back to shore. You can't take it out in the channel."

"That's my problem," Frank snapped. "How much do you want?"

The man shrugged. "Take it. Who knows? Maybe you'll get lucky and catch those jerks. If you do, just remember to bring back our parachute."

"I'll bring it back," Frank promised. "But how will I find you?"

"We'll be here," came the reply. "If we're not, just ask around for Freddie or Mike Ahina. All the locals know us."

Frank bent over the side and untied the lines that secured the jet-ski. He climbed down onto it, holding the side of the boat with one hand to keep steady. He pressed the starter and twisted the throttle on the end of the handlebar. The small engine sounded like an angry swarm of bees.

"Oh, well," Frank told himself. "It sure beats swimming in wet clothes."

Even though the engine wasn't very big, Frank discovered the jet-ski was pretty quick. It was made of lightweight materials and designed to skip across the surface of the water. That was exactly what it did. Every time Frank hit a small wave, the jet-ski flew into the air.

It took some getting used to. It was like waterskiing and motorcycle motocross racing jumbled together. Frank almost lost it a couple times, coming down hard and wobbly on the front ski. But after a while he started shifting his weight whenever the jet-ski took off, keeping the front end up and forcing the back end down.

The water started to get choppy farther out from shore, and it was harder to control the machine. Frank knew it would get a lot worse before it got any better. The volcanic mountains of the islands acted as giant windbreaks, keeping the ocean calm along the coastline. The winds whipped the water into whitecaps out in the interisland channel, though, and that was where the speedboat had gone. So that's where Frank was going, too.

A wave smacked the jet-ski broadside. Frank fought for control. Saltwater sprayed over his face and shoulders. He couldn't jump these waves as he had the smaller ones near shore. They were too big—and getting bigger.

He tried to weave between them. This is like running a marathon in a minefield, Frank thought. Except these mines are moving.

He began to think the Hawaiians had been right—he'd never make it across the channel on the jet-ski. Dodging one wave after another meant he had to swerve off in one direction, then cut back to get on course again, only to veer off again to skirt another whitecap. His chances of catching the speedboat had been slim when he was moving in a straight line. Threading a twisted path through the rolling hills of water didn't exactly improve the odds.

Frank knew he'd never catch them this way. He was about to give up and try to make it back to Maui when he saw a bright shape flashing across the waves. It was a white speedboat, with a ragged streak of crimson on the side.

Frank looked at the red lightning bolt. He couldn't believe his luck. They were almost headed right at him. But where was the parachute? Where was Joe?

Frank pushed those questions out of his mind. One thing at a time. And the first thing, he told himself, is to get on that boat.

He aimed the jet-ski at the oncoming speedboat. Frank held his breath, waiting for them to change course to avoid him, but the speedboat cut a straight line through the water. Frank closed the gap between them. Still no reaction.

Why don't they do something? Frank wondered. Can't they see me? He glanced down at the blue-and-white jet-ski and chuckled. He was wearing a white T-shirt and blue jeans. Perfect camouflage against the blue ocean and the white wave crests.

It suddenly occurred to Frank that he had no idea how he was going to get on the speedboat.

70

They sure weren't going to stop and offer him an invitation. "I'll just have to wing it," he muttered to himself.

A wave started to rise up between Frank and his target. Frank saw his chance. He twisted the knob on the handlebar and hit the swell at full throttle. The jet-ski soared over the crest and became airborne. It hurtled toward the speedboat, but Frank could tell it was going to fall short. The combined weight of Frank and the jet-ski was too much.

So he let go of the handlebars and kicked off with his feet. The jet-ski dropped away, and Frank sailed right above the boat and thudded onto the deck, landing on his side.

There was a sharp pain in his hip, but Frank ignored it. He jumped to his feet and whirled around to face two hulking brutes. Both were wearing dark suits and sunglasses. They definitely didn't look like sailors.

They definitely didn't look Hawaiian, either. The one holding the wheel had short, light brown hair with a small bald spot in the back. He turned and gave Frank a cold, hard stare. "Get rid of him," he growled to his partner.

The second man nodded and reached into his coat, but Frank slammed his foot into the man's stomach before the gun had cleared the shoulder holster. He doubled over from the blow, and Frank's hand came down on the back of his neck with blurring speed. The man slumped to the deck.

Frank didn't stop to admire his work. The thug behind the wheel was turning, starting to make his move. Frank spun around, swinging his left leg up for a roundhouse kick. The side of Frank's foot smashed into the man's jaw. The thug's sunglasses flew off, and his head smacked the steering wheel.

Frank didn't give him a chance to fall. He pushed him up against the side rail and reached inside the man's coat. He felt cold steel and leather and pulled out a .45 automatic pistol. Frank thumbed off the safety and shoved the gun in the man's face.

"Where's my brother?" Frank rasped.

The thug sneered. "You mean the jerk with the girl?"

Frank pressed the gun against the man's skin. "The only jerk I see is the one with the barrel of a forty-five up his nose. Now, where are they? I *won't* ask again."

The man shrugged. "It don't make no difference anyway. There's nothing you can do. They're on Kahoolawe."

"What's wrong?" Joe asked. He was standing on a rocky beach, the parachute bunched up in his arms. "Those guys aren't coming after us. As soon as they saw us land here, they took off. They probably would have ripped the bottom

out of that boat if they tried to bring it in
here."

Jade didn't respond. She had the harness half
off and was staring at a signpost stuck in the
sand. Danger! it warned in big red letters. Keep
Off! Beneath that was a single Hawaiian word,
Kahoolawe.

"Hey," Joe said when he saw the sign. "I
thought you said all the beaches in Hawaii were
public. Who's this Kahoolawe guy?"

Jade turned to him. There was fear in her
eyes. "That's the name of the island," she said.
"The whole thing belongs to the navy."

"So we'll get arrested for trespassing on government property," Joe replied. "It's better than
wrestling with sharks."

Jade shook her head. "You don't understand.
Nobody comes here—not even the navy.

"They use the island only for target practice."

Chapter
9

THE *BIG DEAL* raced toward Maui. Frank had the throttle wide open. Every time the boat hit a wave, the bow reared up out of the water and then crashed back down. Salt spray splashed the windshield.

Frank checked the fuel gauge. Almost empty. Barely enough to make it. If he had tried for Kahoolawe, he would have ended up stranded there with his brother and Jade. He glanced back at his two passengers, firmly tied up with the anchor line.

He pulled into the small marina in the harbor at Lahaina, ignoring the No Wake signs. He killed the engine and let the speedboat drift to the dock. He was already standing on the bow when it scraped against the pier. He jumped off and wrapped the bowline around a post.

"Hey, man!" a voice called out. "Where's our para-sail? You said you'd bring it back."

Frank turned and saw Mike Ahina, his brother Freddie behind him.

Frank nodded at the white speedboat with the red lightning bolt. "I got something almost as good," he replied. "The creeps that stole it."

Frank looked at the two hired thugs bound hand and foot on the deck of the boat. One of them was still out cold. The other was glaring back at him.

Frank turned back to the Hawaiian brothers. "Listen, could you keep an eye on those two until the cops get here? I'll call them right after I get through to Pearl Harbor."

"You know somebody at Pearl?" Freddie asked.

"No," Frank replied. "But my brother's stuck on Kahoolawe, and only the navy can get him off."

"Kahoolawe?" Freddie Ahina said. "You know what they use that island for?"

Frank nodded quickly. "Yeah, but I don't know when they plan to use it next. So I'm kind of in a hurry. Where's the nearest phone?"

Mike Ahina scowled. "You'd just be wasting your time, man. They won't call off a bombing run just because some kid calls them up and tells them to."

Frank looked at him. "You mean they're going to bomb it *today?*"

Freddie shrugged. "They bomb it all the time, but they've got some big exercise going on right now. Lots of battleships out there. Only thing you can know for sure—Kahoolawe's going to get a brutal pounding before it's over."

"Then I've got to get back there now!" Frank burst out.

"I know the fastest way to get you there," Freddie said. "Let me make a call and set it up."

While Freddie Ahina was gone, his brother jumped into the speedboat to check on the two thugs. "Hey, what's this?" he called to Frank. "Looks like a picture of the girl who was with your brother."

"Let me see that," Frank said. It looked like a photocopy of a page torn out of a magazine. It was a picture of Jade all right—but she looked a few years younger. She was holding a surfboard. Standing next to her was her father, Kevin Roberts.

"Where'd you get this?" Frank asked.

"I found it on the deck," the Hawaiian responded.

Ten minutes later a helicopter swooped down out of the sky, hovered for a moment, then settled down gently on the end of the pier. Frank was surprised that the dock could hold all that weight, but he didn't stop to analyze it.

The door of the cockpit swung open. Frank ducked and ran over to it, the rotors whirling just a few feet over his head. He started to climb in, grabbing the door frame with both hands and stepping on the front of the skid bar.

The helicopter wobbled slightly. Frank looked down. The machine wasn't resting on the pier at all. It was hovering just a few inches above it. Frank glanced across the seat at the pilot.

The man flashed a wide grin through his bushy beard. "Welcome to Doyle Island Tours. I'm your pilot, Hank Doyle. Hurry up and get in. I charge by the hour."

Frank clambered into the copilot's seat and strapped himself in. "Let's go," he shouted over the deafening howl of the engine.

Doyle tapped his headset and pointed to a similar unit on a hook on the side of the copilot's seat. Frank put it on. The headphones covered his ears, cutting out some of the noise. A small microphone was attached on one side.

"So you're a friend of Freddie Ahina's?" a voice crackled in Frank's ear.

"Actually I just met him today," Frank admitted.

The pilot turned to him. "You mean I'm supposed to take on the U.S. Navy for some lousy tourist? I owe Freddie a favor, but this is really pushing it. Who are you, anyway?"

Frank looked at him, trying to penetrate Doyle's aviator shades with his gaze. He chose his words carefully. "I'm a guy who needs your help. I can't make you help me—I can't even ask you. I wouldn't ask anybody to risk his life flying into a target area during a naval barrage."

Frank slapped the release button on the shoulder straps of the copilot's seat. "My brother's on Kahoolawe, and that's where I'm going. If you won't take me, I'll figure out some other way to get there."

He started to take off the headset. Doyle's voice came through the earphones. "Hold on a second. You didn't answer my question. Who are you?"

"What difference does it make?" Frank asked.

The pilot grinned. "If we're going to get killed together, we should be on a first-name basis, don't you think?" He took his right hand off the control stick and held it out. "My friends call me Skydog."

Frank grasped Doyle's hand. "Thanks," he sighed. "My name's Frank Hardy. Whatever it costs, I'll find some way to pay you."

Doyle pulled back on the control stick and the helicopter banked up and away from the pier. "Forget it." He laughed. "If I had a dollar for every grunt I pulled out of a fire zone, I'd be a rich man. Besides, I can't stand those armchair admirals and their pretend wars. Somebody should put some howitzers on that island and start shooting back. That'd give them something to put in their reports!''

Frank watched as Doyle worked the controls. It looked a lot like flying an airplane—except there seemed to be an extra lever by the left side of the seat. All of the pilot's controls were also duplicated on the copilot's side. Frank glanced over to his left and saw a lever next to his seat, too. He reached down and touched the handgrip.

"You know anything about flying?" Doyle suddenly asked.

Frank shrugged. "I took a few lessons back home. I could land a single-engine plane if I had to, but this looks a lot trickier."

That was an understatement. The dizzying array of dials, gauges, and switches were a total mystery to Frank.

Doyle nodded. "It takes a special breed to be a chopper jockey. Helicopters can do a lot of things airplanes can't—like hover, fly backward, and take off and land vertically. So they need more controls. It takes two hands and two feet all working together to fly this baby."

He patted the control stick in front of him. "This is the cyclic pitch control. Moving this changes the angle of the main rotor blades. You push it forward and you go forward. You pull it back, and you go backward. Simple, right?"

"So far," Frank replied. "But how do you turn?"

The pilot pointed at his feet. "See those pedals? They control the tail rotor. Press one and you increase the tail rotor thrust, and you turn one way." He pushed down on the left pedal and the helicopter banked to the left. "Press the other, and you decrease the tail thrust."

"And you turn right—right?" Frank said.

"You got it," Doyle replied. "Now all you need to know is how to make it go up and down."

Frank smiled. "I bet that lever next to the seat is the missing ingredient."

"Right again," Doyle said. "That's the collective pitch control. Pull it up, and up we go." He gripped the lever and pulled. The helicopter soared upward.

Then abruptly he pushed the lever down. The helicopter swooped in a steep dive. Frank's stomach felt as if it had just jumped into his throat. He clutched at the control stick in front of him. It was the closest thing he could hang onto.

The bearded pilot eased the lever up, and the helicopter pulled out of the dive just before they hit the water. "Yee-ha!" he yelled. "This is the only way to travel!" The waves rushed by just a few feet beneath them.

Frank realized a good-size swell could easily swamp them. "Shouldn't we pull up a little?" he suggested, trying to sound cool and casual. "Like maybe to an altitude where we might show up on the navy's radar?"

Doyle laughed. "Great idea, kid! Let's take

her up where we can get a real close look at some of those sixteen-inch shells that the sailors like to throw at Kahoolawe.''

''If they know we're here,'' Frank said, ''they won't fire, right?''

''I wouldn't bet my life on it,'' the pilot answered. ''Let's give them a call and see what happens.'' He thumbed a switch on the control panel and spoke into the microphone. ''Mayday! Mayday! This is Victor Able one five niner. We have lost hydraulic pressure and are going down on Kahoolawe.''

There was a long pause. Static hissed through the headset. Then another voice crackled in Frank's ears. ''Ah, say again, Victor Able one five niner. We didn't copy that.''

''Mayday!'' Doyle barked. ''We are making an emergency landing on Kahoolawe!''

There was another static-filled pause, and then, ''Ah, negative on that, Victor Able. You are entering a restricted flight zone. There is a naval exercise in progress. Alter course immediately. Do not, repeat, do *not* land on Kahoolawe.''

The pilot looked at Frank and shrugged. He reached over to the control panel and flipped the radio switch on and off rapidly as he spoke into the microphone. ''Signal breaking up. We did not copy last message. Repeat—we are going down on Kahoolawe. Mayday! Mayday!''

He shut off the radio and turned to Frank.

"Maybe that will confuse them long enough for us to get in and out."

Frank heard a hollow whistling sound, and something whizzed by overhead. He looked at the island ahead and saw a patch of ground erupt in a spray of dirt and smoke.

"I wouldn't bet my life on it," he replied grimly.

Chapter

10

JOE AND JADE huddled beside a small outcropping of rock. The ground shook every time one of the heavy shells exploded. Even though the action seemed to be focused on another part of the island, Joe didn't want to take any chances.

Jade put her hand on his arm. "Tell me again," she said, "about how somebody is going to find us."

Joe listened to the steady *krump krump krump* in the distance. He couldn't tell for sure, but he thought the noise was getting louder.

He patted Jade's hand and pointed to the beach. He had spread the rainbow-colored parachute on the ground, holding down the edges with football-size rocks. "From the air, anybody can see that. It's as good as a flare gun or a signal fire."

A shell exploded close by with a deafening roar that left Joe's ears ringing. Jade's fingernails dug into his arm.

"Tell me how we're going to survive until then!" she shouted.

"That was just a stray shot," Joe tried to reassure her. "They're concentrating all their firepower inland. All we have to do is sit tight."

There was another earsplitting blast nearby. Sand and pulverized rock showered down around them. The air was full of dark smoke and dust.

Frank spotted something down on the rocky beach. He heard the telltale whistling again, and then another chunk of the island was smashed into a rain of pebbles and dust. When the smoke cleared, whatever had been there was gone. Still, he thought it was worth a look.

He tapped the pilot's shoulder and pointed. "Take us down there! I thought I saw something."

Doyle nodded and moved the control stick. The helicopter turned and raced down the shoreline. Frank scanned the beach. Nothing but sand and boulders. A splash of color caught Frank's eye.

"Hold it!" he yelled. "Go back! There is something back there!"

Doyle's feet shifted on the pedals. The helicopter circled around and set down on the rocky beach.

Frank jumped out and picked up a strip of

yellow cloth. There were other scraps of material scattered in the sand. He recognized the rainbow colors of the parachute. There was nothing left but confetti. Frank shuddered. He prayed that Joe and Jade weren't anywhere near the parachute when the explosion ripped into it.

Somebody coughed. Frank whirled and saw a ghost—at least it looked like a ghost. The figure was grayish white from head to toe. It coughed again. "About time you got here," it rasped.

Another dusty figure crawled out from behind a small rock outcropping.

Frank stared at them. "Joe? Jade? Is that you?"

"Who else were you expecting?" Joe replied hoarsely. "The Ghost of Christmas past?"

"You look horrible," Frank gasped. "Are you all right?"

Joe looked down at himself. "Yeah, I think so." He tried to brush off some of the dust, and a small cloud puffed up around him. He coughed again. "I could use a bath, though."

"So where are we going?" Hank Doyle asked after Frank introduced Joe and Jade, and they had flown some distance away from the small, scorched island. "Back to Maui?"

Frank looked at Joe and Jade in the backseat of the helicopter. "We've got to figure out our next move."

"Let's fly back to Oahu," Joe suggested. "We'll go have a little talk with Nick Hawk."

He cracked his knuckles. "I'll give him five or ten good reasons to call off the dogs."

Frank shook his head. "Something tells me this goes way beyond Nick's gambling problems. They were double-teaming us back on Maui—first the guys in the car, and then the two goons in the speedboat."

Joe could see where his brother was leading. "That means somebody with heavy mob connections or a lot of money to burn on hired guns."

"Or both," Frank said.

"So what do we do now?" Jade asked. "We can't stay in this helicopter forever."

"We need to buy some time to come up with a plan," Frank said. "We need a place where nobody can find us for a while."

"I know just the place," the pilot said. He looked at the fuel gauge and tapped it with his finger. "We might just have enough fuel to make it."

"Might?" Joe responded. "What happens if we don't?"

Doyle chuckled. "Then we get wet!" He worked the foot pedals, and the helicopter banked hard to the left.

Frank glanced at the fuel gauge. The needle was still close to *F*. The tank was almost full. Frank smiled. Doyle had a weird sense of humor, but he was beginning to like him. "Cheer up, Joe," he said. "You said you needed a bath, anyway."

They were in the air for over an hour. Frank checked the position of the sun and guessed they were headed northwest. They flew over the small island of Lanai. They saw Molokai in the distance. Oahu passed by on the right. After that, there was nothing but blue for a while. Blue sky above them, and blue ocean below.

Finally a lush, green island loomed ahead.

Jade pointed out the window. "That's Kauai. They call it the garden island. That must be where we're going."

"What makes you think that?" Joe asked.

"Because if it isn't," Doyle answered, "it's an awfully long way to the next island big enough to land on." He turned to Frank and grinned. "Hang on—we're going in hard!"

The helicopter banked to the right and swooped down toward the island. As they got closer, Frank could see a vast, tropical jungle.

"Yee-hah!" the pilot whooped, skimming the tops of the trees. "I love this job! It's the most fun you can have without getting shot at."

Frank spotted a small cabin in a clearing in the jungle. Doyle pulled back on the stick, and the helicopter slowed down. It hovered over the clearing for a moment. Then he pushed down on the lever at his side, and the flying machine eased to the ground.

Doyle cut the engine power and unbuckled his safety harness. "One of the fringe benefits," he said, gesturing at the small cabin surrounded by forest, "is being able to live someplace where you never get uninvited visitors."

They all got out of the helicopter. Joe looked around. Something was missing. "Is there a road anywhere near here?" he asked.

"Depends on what you mean by near—and what you mean by road," Doyle replied. "There's an old dirt trail about a mile from here. I guess you could run a four-wheeler down it."

"So you can get here only by helicopter," Frank said.

"You got it," the pilot answered. He opened the cabin door. "Welcome to Chateau Doyle. Try to ignore the mess. It's been a while since any guests have been here."

They followed him inside. "Looks like it's been a while since *anybody* has been here," Jade said.

There were cobwebs everywhere, and a faint mildew smell filled the air. The sparse wood furniture looked handmade, Frank noticed. Probably carved from trees that grew in the area.

"Well, it has been a while since I was last here," Doyle admitted. "I don't really live here anymore. I just use it as a retreat—a place to chill out when the world gets too weird."

"Like now?" Joe ventured.

A grin spread across the pilot's bearded face.

"Are you kidding? I can't remember the last time I've had so much fun."

"Well, all this fun is making me hungry," Joe said. "I don't suppose you've got anything to eat in the refrigerator. That is, if you have a refrigerator."

Doyle laughed and slapped Joe on the back. "Let me show you the kitchen. We've got all the modern comforts. Refrigerator, stove, trash compactor—"

"Trash compactor?" Jade echoed.

"Sure," Doyle replied. "There's not a lot you can do with garbage. You can either bury it in the yard and end up living next to a dump, or—"

"Or you can haul it away," Frank cut in. "And if you have to carry it away in a helicopter that doesn't have a lot of extra space, a trash compactor makes a lot of sense."

"What do you do for power?" Joe asked. "I bet the electric company doesn't run any lines out here."

"If they did," Doyle answered, "I'd have neighbors pretty soon, and then I'd have to move. There's a diesel generator out back. It's not much, but it'll give us all the power we need. Come on, I'll show you."

He started to walk to the door and then stopped. He scratched his beard. "Of course, it isn't going to start without any fuel in it." He shrugged his shoulders. "Oh well, it doesn't matter. Any food in the refrigerator would be pretty rank by now, anyway. So I'll just have to jump in the old station wagon and drive down to the Food 'n' Fuel."

"You want any company?" Frank asked.

The pilot waved him off as he headed out the door toward the helicopter. "Nah. You just hang loose for a while. I'll be back before you know it."

For the next few hours, while Joe and Jade sat in the cabin, talking, Frank stared out into the forest and reviewed the case. He glanced at his watch finally and started to get worried. Doyle hadn't returned and the sun was getting low in the sky. He doubted that even Skydog could find the cabin in the middle of the jungle in the dark.

Joe didn't notice the time go by—he was too busy talking to Jade. Eventually he did notice that something was bothering his brother. He walked up behind him and put his hand on Frank's shoulder. "What's up?" he asked.

"Doyle should have been back," Frank answered.

Joe shrugged. "Maybe he had too many items for the express check-out lane. Besides, it's given me a chance to find out some interesting things."

"Like what?" Frank replied. "Jade's favorite rock band? Her shoe size?"

Joe put his hand over his heart. "You wound me." He glanced over at the girl and then turned back to his brother. "Let's go outside and get some fresh air." He held the door open for Frank and then followed him out.

"So what'd you find out?" Frank asked.

"Do you know why Jade's father doesn't like her surfing?" Joe answered Frank with another question.

"Because it's dangerous?"

"No. Because of the publicity."

Frank frowned. "Replay that for me."

"When Jade first started to get known in competition, some dinky surfing magazine did a feature on her. She gave them this old picture of herself with her first surfboard. It was a present from her father—and he was in the picture, too. When her old man saw the article, he almost grounded her for life."

Frank pulled a piece of paper out of his pocket. "You mean this picture?"

Joe looked at it. "Where did you get that?"

"Off one of those thugs that took you and Jade for a joyride," Frank replied.

"It all starts to fit together, doesn't it?" Joe said.

"Yeah," Frank agreed. "No family, no past, no publicity—sounds like Kevin Roberts has been on the run for the past fifteen years."

"And whoever he was running from finally caught up with him," Joe added.

Frank looked at his brother. "There's something else bothering me."

"What's that?"

"How did those hoods back on Maui know where to find us?"

The *whup-whup-whup* of a helicopter cut through the air.

"Doyle's back," Joe said.

Frank looked up and spotted the helicopter close by. Something was wrong! It was weaving through the air, its tail swinging from side to side. Then it just dropped.

Chapter

11

FRANK COULD TELL the helicopter was coming down too fast. It hit the ground hard. The landing skid on the left side smashed down first. The struts groaned and buckled. Then the machine rocked the other way. The right skid smacked the ground, bounced up, and finally settled down.

The whine of the engine died down. Frank and Joe bolted toward the cockpit. Frank yanked open the door. Hank Doyle grinned out at him. "Sorry I'm late," he said. The smile wavered. "But the traffic was murder."

Frank poked his head into the cockpit. "Are you okay?" he asked the pilot.

Doyle nodded. "Yeah, but I think I've dodged enough artillery for one day."

Joe peered in over his brother's shoulder and

saw a single bullet hole in the windshield. "Something tells me this isn't the work of a disgruntled customer," he said. "So maybe you should tell us exactly what happened."

"I flew back to Maui to pick up some gear. A guy showed up at the hangar just as I was getting ready to head back here," Doyle replied. "He wanted to know where you were. I made a break for it, but he managed to shoot off a couple rounds before I got the chopper off the ground."

"Why'd you come all the way back here?" Frank asked. "Why not just head for the nearest police station?"

Doyle snorted. "Because he *was* the police. He flashed an FBI badge at me before he started asking questions."

"FBI?" Joe echoed. "What did he look like?"

The pilot shrugged his shoulders. "He looked like a fed."

"That's it?" Frank prodded. "No distinguishing marks?"

"Oh, yeah," Doyle said. "He had a scar over his left eye. Do you know him?"

"We ran into him once before," Joe replied.

"I have a bad feeling we'll tangle with him again before this is over," Frank said grimly.

He glanced around the inside of the helicopter. Other than the bullet hole in the windshield, there were no signs of damage. "Will this thing still fly?" he asked.

Doyle chuckled. "I got here, didn't I?"

"Just barely," Frank noted.

"The tail rotor controls are kind of stiff," Doyle admitted. "He must have hit one of the cables. But it's nothing I can't handle."

Frank turned to his brother. "Get Jade. We're leaving now. We've got to get back to Honolulu right away."

"Right," Joe said. "No wonder those goons were right behind us every step of the way. Every time you called Dad, that FBI agent tipped them off."

"If they knew where to find us," Frank added, "how long do you think it will take them to track down Jade's father?"

As the helicopter flew across the water, Joe told Jade what they had pieced together.

"Who was my father hiding from?" she asked. "What did he do?"

"We don't know," Joe said. "But a safe bet would be that it has something to do with the mob and the FBI—and it happened a long time ago."

"You mean before we moved to Hawaii," Jade said.

Joe nodded. "The government might even have relocated you as part of the witness protection program."

"It doesn't make any sense!" she protested. "Why now—after fifteen years? You can't tell me they've been looking for us all this time!"

"It does sound kind of farfetched, doesn't it?" Joe admitted. "But maybe they weren't looking at all. Maybe they just stumbled across you by accident."

Jade's shoulders slumped. "It's all my fault."

Joe reached out and took her hand. "You were only two when it happened—whatever it was. How could it be your fault?"

"The magazine article," she said. "No wonder my father was so upset."

"You had no way of knowing," Joe assured her.

She turned and looked at him. "What do we do now?"

"We fly to Waikiki," Joe explained, "and grab your father out of the hotel before anybody else finds out he's there."

"And then?" she asked.

Joe cleared his throat. "We're still working on that part."

"How do you know we're not already too late?" she pressed.

Joe didn't answer right away. He looked into her green eyes. "We don't," he finally said. "But we've got to try, right?"

The sun had set, and a full moon sparkled on the water. The only other source of light lay straight ahead. "That's Honolulu," Doyle announced. "I'll take her down over Waikiki Beach. But you're going to have to jump the last couple of feet—I can't risk landing more than once on that skid I busted back on Kauai."

"After we jump," Frank said, "you better get out of here. I don't know what we'll run into, and I don't want you to get stuck in the middle again."

The pilot grinned. "I like the fireworks. They make me feel alive, but I don't think I'll be much help in this crippled chopper. We're coming up on the beach now. Get ready to bail out."

The helicopter hovered a few feet above the sand. Joe pushed the back door open and jumped down. Jade stood in the opening. Joe reached out, and she jumped into his arms.

Frank watched to make sure they were all right. Then he turned to the pilot. "I don't know how to thank you for all you've done," he said.

"I'd send you a bill," Doyle replied, "but I don't have your address. Now, get out of here so I can go find some paying customers."

Frank opened the door and climbed out. The wind from the rotor blades whipped his hair around, and he had to shield his eyes from the blowing sand that pelted him. He flashed a thumbs-up gesture to the pilot, and the machine lifted off. Frank ran up the beach to join his brother.

Frank led the way back to the hotel through the beach entrance. When he walked into the hotel suite, the first thing he saw was his father sitting at the writing desk.

When Fenton Hardy saw his son standing in the doorway, he said, "I thought you were still on Maui. Why didn't you call and let me know you were coming back here?"

"It's a long story," Frank said.

"A very long story," Joe chimed in.

"Well, I dug up quite a story of my own," Fenton replied. He looked at Jade. "I got most of it from your father."

"Does it have anything to do with the witness protection program?" she asked.

Fenton looked surprised. "He told me you didn't know anything about it."

"She didn't," Joe said. "We just put it all together today."

"But we don't have any of the details," Frank added. "How about filling in the gaps for us?"

"Sixteen years ago," Fenton began, "an undercover FBI agent penetrated the heart of a West Coast mob bookmaking and loan-sharking operation. They took bets on anything and everything. They'd even lend you the money to bet with."

"Then break your legs if you couldn't pay them back," Joe said.

His father nodded. "Something like that. Anyway, this undercover agent broke the whole case wide open. His testimony sent the ringleader, Thomas Catlin, to prison. Catlin swore he'd get revenge.

"But criminals make threats like that all the

time," he continued. "Nobody took it seriously until a bomb demolished the agent's house. The agent was in a nearby park with his daughter when it happened. The only person in the house was his wife."

"My mother," Jade whispered.

"I'm afraid so," Fenton replied. "She was killed instantly. After that, you and your father got new identities and moved to Hawaii to start a new life. It should have ended there. But two years ago Catlin got out of prison and took up where he left off. About a year ago he started expanding his operation into the islands."

"Wait a minute," Frank cut in. "Jade's father couldn't have known that."

"He didn't," Fenton said. "Until I told him. That's why he came to me—the Bureau told him I was his contact. That's the real reason I'm in Hawaii. Catlin imported some heavy talent from New York. I've busted a couple of them before, and I know how they work. So I was brought in as an adviser."

He turned to his sons. "All this is strictly classified information. Top secret."

"I'm afraid it's not much of a secret anymore," Joe replied.

"What do you mean?" his father asked.

"He means somebody inside the FBI is working for Catlin," Frank said. "Every time I called to let you know where we were, a couple of trained gorillas homed in on us."

Fenton Hardy frowned. "The only person I told was Pete Gordon, the special agent I've been working with."

"I don't suppose this Gordon guy has a scar over his left eye," Joe said.

"Yes," Fenton replied. "How did you know?"

"Because a friend of ours saw him on Maui late this afternoon, trying to track Jade down," Frank explained.

All the color drained out of Fenton's face, and he slumped back in his chair. "Then it looks like we've got a very serious situation," he said gravely. "Gordon was supposed to be out setting up a safe house this afternoon—a place for Jade and her father to stay awhile."

"So we'll just get them out of here now," Joe said.

"Where *is* my father?" Jade asked. "He's all right, isn't he?"

Fenton Hardy raised his eyes slowly to meet hers. "I'm sorry," he said. "I didn't know. Gordon picked him up an hour ago."

Chapter

12

"WE'VE GOT TO GET Jade out of here," Frank said. "They could be back looking for her here. This is the most logical place for us to bring her."

Jade slumped down in a chair. "Why would they want me?" she asked glumly, staring at the floor. "They got what they wanted—my father."

"I'm not so sure about that," Frank answered. "They could have grabbed him anytime. Why now?"

Joe thought about it for a minute. "Because they couldn't get Jade."

Frank nodded. "All this time they've been trying to get her, not him."

Jade looked up. "But why?"

"I don't have the answer to that one," Frank

said. "But I think I may know someone who does."

He turned to his father. "Are the police still holding Nick Hawk?"

Fenton shook his head. "They didn't have any solid evidence. After we found out about Kevin Roberts's connection to Catlin, that shifted the attention away from Hawk."

Joe glanced at his brother. "I don't get it. Do you think Hawk is mixed up with Catlin?"

"Think about it," Frank said. "Catlin's a king-pin of bookies and loan sharks—and Nick Hawk has some heavy gambling debts."

"Let's go find out what he knows," Joe said, glancing over at Jade. "Do you know where Nick lives?"

She nodded slowly. "I'll take you there."

Joe put his hand on her shoulder. "No, it's too dangerous. We'll have to find a safe place for you to stay before we go after Hawk."

There was a knock at the door. Frank's eyes narrowed. He put a finger to his lips and stepped silently to the door. He peered through the tiny peephole. He wasn't surprised by what he saw. He could clearly see the scar over the man's left eye. He tiptoed back to the others.

"It's Gordon," he whispered.

There was another knock on the door, this time sounding harder, more insistent.

Joe's eyes darted around the room. They stopped at the balcony overlooking the ocean.

"There's only one other way out of here," he said in a low voice.

Fenton Hardy looked at the balcony. "Go for it," he said. "I'll try to buy you some time."

Joe glanced at Frank. His brother nodded. Joe took Jade's hand and led her out onto the balcony. He gripped the railing and looked over the edge. There was another balcony on the next floor down. But a misstep of a few inches would send him plummeting twenty-five floors to the ground. He took a deep breath and climbed over the railing.

He eased himself down until he was hanging from the bottom of the railing. His toes just barely touched the railing of the balcony below. But he couldn't get a solid footing.

The knock on the door changed to pounding. "Just a second!" Fenton Hardy called out. "I was in the shower! I'll be right there!" He had wet his hair in the sink and was now slicking it back.

Joe pumped his legs and started to sway back and forth. He let go of the railing as he swung in toward the lower balcony. Both his feet landed solidly on the cement floor.

Jade followed Joe. He grabbed her around the waist as she dangled from the railing, and pulled her safely in.

Above them, Frank glanced back at his father. "Go ahead," Fenton urged him. "As long as

Gordon doesn't think I suspect anything, I'll be all right.''

Frank grasped the railing with both hands and vaulted into the air. He swung over and down and dropped onto the balcony below.

There was no one else there. Joe and Jade were gone. The sliding glass door that led into the dark hotel room was open, but all the lights were out. Frank poked his head inside. "Joe?" he whispered. "Where are you?"

Someone grabbed his shirt collar and yanked him through the doorway. "Gotcha!" a voice said. It was Joe.

"What's the big idea?" Frank replied. He could barely make out his brother's features in the dim light.

Joe held something up. The moonlight filtering into the room glinted off the surface. It was a heavy, glass ashtray. "If anybody but you had come through that door, they would've gotten it."

"Well, let's get out of here," Frank said, moving toward the front door. He peered around in the gloom. "Where's Jade?"

"Right behind you," came the reply.

Frank whirled around. Jade was standing behind him, a table lamp in her hands.

Frank chuckled softly.

"What's so funny?" Jade asked.

"I was just thinking," Frank answered. "Most couples wait at least a week to start throwing furniture around."

Jade glanced at Joe. "Just ignore him," Joe said. "He was born with a crippling handicap—no sense of humor." He poked his brother in the ribs with the ashtray. "Come on. Let's get out of here."

They drove away from the hotel in Jade's faded green jeep. Joe tried to persuade her to give him the keys. He didn't want her to be there when they questioned Nick Hawk, but she wouldn't budge. She insisted on driving. "It's my car, and it's my life," she stated flatly. "You never would have found his house without me," she added as she pulled over to the curb.

"We'll take it from here," Frank said. "Which house is it?"

"The white bungalow with the palm tree in the yard," she replied.

Joe looked around. In the dark, all the houses looked like white bungalows with palm trees in the yard. But only one of them had a half-dozen surfboards lined up on the front porch.

Jade started to get out of the jeep. Joe pushed her back down gently but firmly. "No," he said. "This is as far as you go. If there's any trouble, you take off as fast as this bucket of bolts will go. Understand?"

She looked up at him. "Joe, I'm responsible. If anything happens to my father . . ." Her voice trailed off.

"Getting yourself hurt isn't going to help your father," Joe pointed out.

"And standing around talking isn't going to help much, either," Frank cut in. "Take a look over there."

In the harsh glow of the porch light, Joe saw a tanned figure with long blond hair. He had a suitcase in one hand and a backpack slung over his shoulder. It was Nick Hawk.

"Looks like Nick's going on a long trip," Frank noted. "And just before the big competition, too."

"Those bags look kind of heavy," Joe said. "Let's give him a hand." He walked quickly across the street, Frank following.

Frank put his hand on his brother's shoulder. "Slow down. Stay cool. He doesn't know who we are. We can take him by surprise."

Nick Hawk was throwing the suitcase and the backpack into the trunk of his car when Frank and Joe strolled up behind him. "Going on a trip?" Frank asked casually.

Hawk spun around. There was a switchblade in his hand. Frank could see that he was wound up tight. The blond surfer sized up the two brothers. "You guys don't work for Catlin," he said mostly to himself. "And you sure aren't cops. Who are you? What do you want?"

"We want some answers," Joe snapped. "And we don't have time to play around. So if you're going to use that blade, make your move now. I'd love an excuse to break your arm."

Hawk's arm dropped to his side. "I can't take much more of this," he said wearily. "You're the two guys that have been hanging around with Jade, aren't you?"

Frank nodded.

"I saw you once and Connie told me about you," the blond surfer continued.

"You mentioned the name Catlin earlier," Frank said. "Do you know Thomas Catlin?"

"Not personally," Hawk replied. "He controls half the bookies on the island, and I owe money to most of them."

"So that means you were in debt to Catlin," Joe said.

Hawk nodded. "He sent one of his trained gorillas to tell me I could pay off the debt with one little job. All I had to do was make sure Jade didn't compete at the Banzai Pipeline."

"So you tried to kill her just to pay off a gangster?" Joe burst out.

The surfer shook his head. "I just wanted to scare her off. I'd never kill her."

"The runaway surfboard at Waikiki and the shooting at Waimea," Frank said. "That was you, right?"

Nick Hawk stared at the ground. "I was desperate. These guys play rough, and they play for keeps. But after I found out I almost shot Connie, I just couldn't go through with it. So I sent word to Catlin that I would find some other way to pay him back.''

''Now you're leaving town before his goons come knocking on your door,'' Joe said.

Hawk looked at him. ''I got a phone call a little while ago. It was Thomas Catlin himself. He told me the debt wouldn't be paid until Jade was dead—or I was.''

''Did he say anything else?'' Frank prodded. ''Anything about Kevin Roberts?''

''Jade's father?'' Hawk replied. He shook his head. ''No, nothing about him. But he did say something weird.''

''What was that?'' Frank asked.

''Catlin said *his* daughter had been waiting a long time for this, but Catlin doesn't have any kids.''

Joe looked at the surfer. ''So what are you going to do now? Run away?''

Nick Hawk shook his head slowly. ''I was— but I guess I owe Jade more than that. Maybe it's time I told the police what really went down.''

''Not yet,'' Frank said. ''Not until Jade and her father are safe.''

''What did Nick say?'' Jade asked when Frank and Joe got back to the jeep. ''Anything that'll help?''

''We don't know yet,'' Joe answered vaguely. He didn't think it would help Jade to hear proof of Catlin's grisly intentions. "We still don't have all the pieces."

Frank yawned in the backseat. "We're not going to find any of them tonight. We need to find a place to get a few hours' sleep."

"We can go to Al Kealoha's house," Jade suggested. "I know we can trust him."

"Sounds good to me," Joe said. "Let's go."

"Stop at the gas station up ahead on the right," Frank said. "I want to call the hotel and make sure Dad's all right."

The telephone rang a few times before someone answered. "Hotel operator," a voice said.

"Give me room twenty-five-fifteen, please," Frank said.

"One moment," came the reply.

There was a strange clicking and humming on the line. Frank didn't know if it was a problem with the pay phone or the hotel switchboard. Finally, he heard his father's voice. "Hello?" Fenton said. "Who is this?"

"It's me," Frank said.

"Frank?" Fenton replied. "Are you all right?"

"Everybody's fine," Frank assured him. "We're going—"

"Don't tell me where you are or where you're going," his father cut in. "There may be a tap on this line."

As soon as Frank hung up, the pay phone rang. He stared at it for a moment. It kept ringing. He picked it up.

"I hope you get a good night's rest," a voice murmured in the receiver. It sounded like a man with ice water in his veins. It sounded like Pete Gordon. "Because tomorrow morning at eight o'clock sharp you're going to deliver the girl to me at Sand Island Park."

"What if we don't show?" Frank snapped. "What can you do about it?"

"We can kill Kevin Roberts," came the cold reply. "Very slowly—and *very* painfully."

Chapter

13

FRANK DIDN'T SAY ANYTHING about Gordon's threat when he got back in the jeep. He wanted to talk to Joe alone before telling Jade. He finally got his chance when they got to Al Kealoha's house.

"You guys don't mind waiting here a minute, do you?" Jade asked. "Let me just talk to Al alone first and make sure it's all right."

"No problem," Frank replied. "Take your time." After she was gone, he turned to his brother and said, "We've got a problem. We're running out of time."

"So what's our next move?" Joe asked after Frank told him about the phone call.

Frank looked at his watch. "I don't know—

but we've only got about eight hours to come up with something."

Jade waved to Frank and Joe from the front porch of the house. They got out of the jeep and joined her.

Al Kealoha was standing in the doorway. The big Hawaiian surfer studied the Hardys for a moment. "Jade tells me you guys saved her life," he finally said. "I also saw what you did for Connie after that wipeout at Waimea. You can stay here as long as you want. Anything you need, just ask."

They followed him inside. Joe looked around and saw electronic equipment everywhere. Televisions, radios, videocassette recorders, even a couple of microwave ovens.

"How about a stereo?" he asked.

Al Kealoha smiled. "Don't get the wrong idea. This stuff didn't fall off a truck. Most of them are broken. Like this TV here. I buy it cheap, fix it up, and sell it. Surfing's my life, but it doesn't pay the rent."

Joe picked up a remote control for a garage door opener. "This isn't worth much all by itself."

"You'd be surprised," Kealoha replied. "You can change the radio frequency so that it works with almost any garage door opener."

Frank was inspecting a digital clock that showed the time as 88:88. He looked up at the Hawaiian. "What did you say?"

"I said you can change the radio frequency so—"

"That's what I thought you said," Frank cut in. "You wouldn't happen to have an old radar detector around here, would you?"

"I had a couple," Kealoha said. "But they go fast. Maybe there's still one around somewhere."

The Hawaiian poked around inside a few cardboard boxes. "Got one," he finally said, holding up a small, black object.

"What are you going to do with it?" Jade asked.

"I'll tell you in the morning," Frank said. "But right now, you should get some sleep. I have a feeling tomorrow's going to be a long day."

It was still pitch black out when Joe woke up. He hadn't meant to fall asleep at all. He had dozed off in a chair while his brother and Al Kealoha puttered around with the insides of the garage door remote control and the radar detector. He glanced at a clock on the table. He thought he must still be asleep. According to the clock, the time was 88:88.

"What time is it?" he asked groggily.

Frank looked at his watch. "A little after two."

"How much longer?" Joe wanted to know.

"Almost got it," Frank replied. He took the back-plate from the remote control and screwed it back in place. "Okay, Al—ready?"

"Go ahead," came the reply. "Hit the switch."

Frank aimed the remote control at the radar detector on the workbench across the room. He pressed the wide, rectangular button on the top. "Take that," he whispered.

The tiny red light on the radar detector winked on. Frank watched the numbers climb in the LED readout next to the indicator light: 2—3—4—5. The display held steady at 5. Frank moved the remote control slightly to one side. The numbers started to fall. He waved it back, and they rose again. He took his thumb off the button, and the red light on the radar detector winked off.

"It works!" he shouted.

Joe put a finger to his lips. "Shhh! You'll wake up Jade!"

"It works!" Frank whispered excitedly. "You know what this means?"

The big Hawaiian smiled sleepily. "Yeah, it means we can go to bed now."

Frank aimed the remote control and pushed the button again. The light on the radar detector glowed red. "It also means we now have a radio homing device."

The next time Joe woke up it was because the sun was shining in his eyes. He sat up and squinted out the window. It looked like it was going to be another perfect day in paradise. Then he remembered they had an appointment, and suddenly the sun didn't seem so warm and bright anymore.

Al Kealoha was fast asleep in another chair. Frank was curled up on the couch, eyes shut tight. Joe shook his brother's shoulder. "Come on," he said. He grabbed Frank's wrist and checked the watch strapped to it. "It's six-thirty. We've got to roll."

The bedroom door swung open, and Jade shuffled out. "What's going on?" she asked.

Joe looked over at her. He didn't have the heart to tell her, but he didn't have the stomach to lie either. "Just give us a few more hours," he said. "Then I'll explain everything. Okay?"

She frowned. "Do I have any choice?"

"Not really," Frank mumbled as he got up from the couch. He picked up the modified remote control and the radar detector and grabbed a roll of black electrical tape off the workbench.

"Just a few more hours," Joe repeated as they headed out the door.

"Where are you going without a car?" Jade called out.

Joe gave her a sheepish grin and held up a set of car keys.

"How'd you get those?" she demanded.

"I kind of borrowed them from your purse while you were sleeping," he told her.

As the Hardys drove away in the jeep, Joe watched Jade in the rearview mirror. She was standing in the doorway, hands on her hips. She looked beautiful. He hoped he'd get a chance to see her again. Reluctantly he shifted his gaze to the road ahead. They had a job to do, but first he had to make sure they got there in one piece.

He glanced at his brother sitting in the passenger seat next to him. "What do you think Gordon will do when he finds out we didn't bring Jade?"

"That's my problem," Frank said. He was busy wrapping electrical tape around the garage door remote control. "He's not even going to see you."

Frank wound the tape tightly over the wide button, making sure it was pressed down firmly. He kept the tape clear of the front end of the unit so it wouldn't interfere with the signal. After he was satisfied that the tape would prevent the button from popping up, he tore a few more long strips off the roll. He stuck them on the remote control unit, but he didn't wind them around it. Instead he left them dangling down like long, black spider legs.

"There's the entrance to the park," Joe said. "Are you ready?"

Frank switched on the radar detector and aimed the remote control unit at it. The red light glowed and the numbers crawled upward. He checked his watch. It was seven-fifteen. "Ready as I'll ever be," he answered grimly.

Joe drove into the empty parking lot. "There's only one thing wrong with this plan," he said.

Frank nodded. "We don't know where Gordon will park." He looked around the parking lot. On one side, it was bordered by a small, open field. On the other, there were bushes and trees crowding in close to the pavement.

Frank pointed toward the bushes. "Park over on that side."

Joe backed into a space, and they got out of the jeep. Joe walked over to the bushes. "These will give me plenty of cover—*if* Gordon parks on this side, too."

Frank shook his head. "Gordon won't park here. He's cautious. He'll suspect a trap." Frank gestured toward the field. "He'll pull in over there."

"But there's no place to hide over there," Joe protested.

"Sure there is," Frank replied. He pointed at a large garbage can, sitting alone in the clearing. "Right there."

Joe glanced at his brother. "Why do I always let *you* come up with the plans?" he muttered.

"You don't have to get *in* it," Frank said. "Just crouch down behind it. And don't forget this." He handed Joe the remote control wrapped in electrical tape.

Joe had barely gotten into position when a black van rolled into the parking lot. Frank checked his watch again. It was only seventhirty. Gordon had shown up early, too.

Frank leaned against the hood of the jeep and

waited. The van paused in the entrance, and then slowly angled over to the far side of the lot, next to the clearing. A faint smile passed over Frank's lips.

Pete Gordon stepped out of the van. He glanced over at Frank. Then he turned around slowly, surveying the entire area. Finally his cold gaze returned to the jeep. He took a few steps forward to get a better look. "Where's your brother?" he asked.

Joe watched the rogue FBI agent step away from the van. It was time to make his move. He edged out from behind the garbage can and darted over to the van.

Frank kept his eyes on Gordon. "He couldn't make it," he said coolly. "He had other plans."

Gordon came closer. "Where's the girl?"

Frank shrugged. "She couldn't make it, either."

Joe slid under the side of the van and slapped the remote control unit onto its underside, using the long strips of tape to hold it in place. Then he quietly sneaked back to his hiding spot.

"You just signed Kevin Roberts's death warrant," Gordon growled.

Frank looked him right in the eye. "I don't think so. If you wanted to kill him, he'd be dead already."

The agent glared at him. "I'll give you two hours to change your mind. If you're not back here with the girl by then, the old man dies."

"I don't know if I could even *find* her in two

hours," Frank replied. "My brother took off with her. I don't know where they are."

"Six hours, then," Gordon hissed. "No more. Tell the girl. Let her decide."

He spun around and strode back to the van. He opened the door and paused. He was looking at the open field. Had he seen something? Frank couldn't tell.

Suddenly Gordon whirled around and pointed a gun right at Frank. There was a fat silencer on the end of the barrel. One side of Gordon's mouth curled up in a menacing sneer. "Sorry, kid," he called out. "I just can't trust you."

Chapter

14

THERE WAS A SOFT *thwump* and then a loud *blam*—right beside Frank's foot. The sudden noise made him jump. He spun around and saw the right front tire in shreds.

Gordon was laughing as he got back in the van. He pulled up next to Frank and leaned out the window. "Looks like you've got a flat tire," he said. "I hope you weren't planning on following me or anything like that." He laughed again and drove away.

As soon as the van was gone, Joe raced across the parking lot to inspect the damage. Frank was already unbolting the spare tire with a lug wrench. Joe grabbed the jack and stuck it under the front bumper. By the time Frank had the spare off its mounting, Joe already had the front end jacked up.

Two minutes later, they were ready to roll again. "We make a pretty good pit crew," Joe said as he cranked up the engine. "All we need now is a good race car."

Frank switched on the radar detector. He looked at the digital display and frowned. "Looks like we're going to need one if we want to catch Gordon. He's too far away. I'm not getting any signal."

"Hold on," Joe replied. "I'll get a signal." He slammed his foot down on the gas pedal and the jeep swerved out of the parking lot.

Joe peered up the road. There was no sign of the black van. "He must have turned off somewhere," he said.

"The only question is, where," Frank replied.

Joe shrugged his shoulders. "One street's as good as another." He turned the wheel suddenly, and the jeep veered off onto another street. There was still no sign of the van. Joe pressed down on the gas pedal, and the old jeep picked up speed.

Frank glanced over at the speedometer. It was edging past 50 MPH.

"Don't worry," Joe said. "You'll pick up any speed traps with the radar detector."

"We altered the frequency on both units," Frank replied. "This will only register the signal from the remote control."

"So are you getting anything yet?" Joe asked.

Frank shook his head. "Nothing."

Joe made another sharp turn.

"Where are you going now?" his brother asked.

"To the Pali Highway," Joe responded. "Gordon picked the opposite side of the parking lot, why not the other side of the island, too?"

Frank thought about it for a moment and nodded. "It's possible. Anyway, we'll cover more ground that way. If we get within a half mile of that garage door opener, this thing should light up like a Christmas tree."

The jeep chugged up the steep highway and over the mountain pass. Joe kept his eyes on the road ahead, and Frank kept his on the radar detector. There was no sign of the black van and no sign of life from the little black box in Frank's lap.

They drove down into the town of Kailua. Frank studied his brother. There was fierce determination in Joe's eyes, but Frank knew there was almost no hope of finding the renegade FBI agent now.

Frank turned away and gazed out at the town.

"What's that?" Joe asked excitedly.

"What's what?" Frank replied.

"The box!" Joe exclaimed. "The light's on!"

Frank picked up the radar detector. Sure enough, the red light was glowing. The digital readout registered 2—3—2—1. Then it was gone, and the light blinked off.

"Go back!" Frank shouted.

Joe slammed on the brakes and threw the jeep into reverse. He backed up to a side street they had just passed, and the red indicator light winked on again.

"Go down this way," Frank gestured.

They followed the winding road. As they slowly went downhill, the glowing numbers on the front of the black box climbed. The road ended at an ornate iron gate. Through the gate Joe could see a huge mansion at the end of a long driveway. Beyond that was the ocean.

Frank scanned the area. The compound appeared to be surrounded on three sides by a high brick wall. He nudged Joe and pointed to the top of the wall. Video surveillance cameras, silently rotating back and forth, cast a sleepless eye over the entire perimeter.

"This must be the place," Joe said.

Frank nodded. "Now all we have to do is figure out how to get in and out without being seen."

Joe shrugged. "I always wanted to be on television."

"How about on a game show where they shoot the losers?" Frank replied.

"Okay," Joe said. "Then we can approach it from the beach. It doesn't look like there are any cameras down there."

Frank shook his head. "They'd see us coming a mile away."

"Maybe," Joe said. "But maybe a few *surfers* wouldn't attract too much attention."

Back at Al Kealoha's house, Jade was sitting on the front steps, waiting for them. Her elbows were on her knees, her chin resting in her hands. Joe had hoped to keep her out of danger, but now they needed her help to save her father.

Joe got out of the jeep and walked up to her. He reached down, took her hand, and pulled her to her feet. "Come on," he said. "Let's go get your father."

Jade looked into his eyes. "Really?" she said hopefully. "You know where he is?"

Joe nodded silently.

"Let's talk about it inside," Frank said. "We're going to need Al's help, too—and anybody else's."

After Frank and Joe laid out their plan, Al got out a map of Kailua. "It's not going to be easy," he said, pointing to the cove where the mansion was located. "There's a small beach—but it's cut off by cliffs on both sides. We'll have to hit the water about a half mile away and paddle the rest of the way."

"Won't they see us coming?" Jade asked.

"That's why we need as many surfers as we can get," Frank answered.

Joe smiled. "We're just a bunch of surf punks looking for a good beach for a party."

The big Hawaiian ran his hand through his

dark, curly hair. "Kind of short notice. How much time do we have?"

Frank checked his watch. "Three hours at the outside."

Kealoha frowned. "Almost everybody's up on the north shore. That's a long drive. The only person in town today is Connie. This is one of the days she works as a waitress."

Jade shook her head. "I don't want to drag Connie into this."

"You don't have any choice," a voice called out.

Frank whirled and saw Connie Lo standing in the doorway. "How did you know we were here?" he asked.

Connie shrugged. "I didn't. Nick told me everything last night. I wanted to help, and I figured Al would, too. Looks like I figured right."

Joe didn't give Jade a chance to argue. "And you're just in time for a little surprise beach party," he said to Connie. "Come on in. We were just about to get out the paper hats and the noisemakers."

On a lonely stretch of windswept beach, they unloaded five surfboards from Jade's jeep and Connie's car. Joe glanced over at Frank and grinned.

Frank shot him a look. "What are you smirking about?"

"I was just thinking," Joe said, his grin widening. "None of those old beach movies was ever anything like this."

"Yeah," Frank replied. "The stars never did any real surfing."

"Just follow my lead," Jade said, "and don't try anything fancy."

"You mean I don't get to hang ten?" Joe said in mock disappointment.

"Get with the program," Connie said. "*Nobody* does that anymore."

They waded out into the water and paddled the surfboards out past a rocky point. On the other side of the point, Joe spotted the mansion nestled in the small cove. He let out a sigh of relief—the beach was deserted. There wasn't a guard or video camera in sight.

Jade paddled over next to him. "Ready to ride your first wave?" she asked.

"Sure," Joe said. "Do we get to shoot the tube?"

"*You* don't even get to do a bottom turn," she answered. "Just wait for the wave and ride it straight in. I'll be right next to you all the way."

Joe could see Frank between the other two surfers. He guessed his brother was probably getting the same instructions.

"Get ready," Jade said. She pointed the board toward the shore. Joe did the same. He glanced over at her. She was intently watching the ocean behind them. "When I give the word," she said, "start paddling like crazy."

Joe could feel the water swelling up under the surfboard.

"Now!" Jade shouted. Her hands splashed into the water, and she shot ahead of him.

Joe felt the building wave rolling in beneath him. He suddenly realized that it was going to roll right on by him unless he got moving. He put on a burst of speed, his arms windmilling through the water. He managed to catch up with Jade just as she stopped paddling.

The next moment she was on her feet. "Come on," she urged. "This is it!"

The wave was just starting to crest as Joe tried to stand. He almost lost his balance, his arms waving around crazily. But then he remembered what Jade had said on that first day. Get the *feel* of it, he reminded himself. He stopped trying to fight the surfboard. He loosened up and let his body flow with it. He was surfing.

His growing smile of satisfaction froze on his lips when he looked toward shore, though. A man ran out of the mansion toward the beach. In one hand he had what looked like a walkie-talkie.

If he had any doubts about what the guy held in his other hand, they were shattered by the sharp crack of gunfire.

Chapter

15

FRANK KNEW that they would run into some kind of reception committee, but he didn't expect them to just start shooting wildly. Luckily, there was only one guard, and he had only fired a warning shot.

Al Kealoha reached the shore first, Connie Lo a moment later. By the time Frank hit the beach, the guard already had the two surfers covered.

Frank could tell the man was nervous. He wasn't prepared for an invasion of surfers. He spotted Frank and started waving the gun around, not sure where to point it.

Frank approached him, smiling and holding his hands up. "What's the problem?"

The guard turned toward him. "Hold it, right there!" he barked.

"Hold what?" the big Hawaiian asked. "There's no law against surfing, is there?"

"And this is a public beach, right?" Connie Lo added.

The man eyed them nervously. "What are you doing here?" he asked sharply.

"Relax," a voice from behind him answered. "We're just here for a little beach party."

The guard whirled around to face the new threat. It was Joe.

"What's going on down there?" a voice crackled over the walkie-talkie in the guard's hand. He stared down at it blankly for a second.

A second was all Frank needed. He grabbed the guard's other arm from behind and yanked it back. He squeezed the wrist and twisted it sharply. The man cried out as he lost his grip on the gun.

The two-way radio squawked again. "What's going on?" it blared. Joe's fist smashed into the guard's face before he could respond. He fell to his knees. Frank let go of his arm, and the man pitched face first into the sand, out cold.

"What's the trouble?" the radio crackled.

Joe bent down and pried it out of the guard's hand. "No trouble," he answered. "Everything's under control."

Frank picked up the gun and handed it to Al Kealoha. Looking at the three surfers, he said, "You guys stay here. Joe and I will go in alone."

"Wait a minute," Jade said. "It's my father in there. I should go."

Joe shook his head. "Too risky." He looked deep into her green eyes. "If he's in there, we'll get him out. I promise."

They reached the house without running into anybody else. The back door was wide open. The guard hadn't bothered to close it in his rush to intercept the surfers. Frank and Joe glanced at each other.

"It could be a trap," Frank said.

Joe shrugged. "There's only one way to find out." He walked through the doorway, and his brother followed.

Joe moved quietly through the kitchen and a large formal dining room. He stopped suddenly when his shoes hit the marble floor of the front hall, and Frank almost bumped into him. The sound of their footsteps echoed in the large entranceway.

"Looks like crime pays pretty well for some guys," Joe said in a low voice.

The place seemed deserted. Joe cocked his head to one side. He thought he heard a faint noise upstairs. He motioned to a wide, curved stairway, and Frank nodded. He had heard it, too.

"Vinnie!" a voice suddenly blared out right next to Joe. "Where are you? What's going on?"

Joe looked down at the forgotten walkie-talkie he had been carrying the whole time. He held it close to his mouth and pushed the talk button. "Ah—I'm still down on the beach. You should come down, too. The water's great!"

"What?" came the startled reply. Joe thought it sounded like stereo. He heard it coming from the two-way radio and from the second floor.

"Never mind," he muttered as he switched off the unit and set it down on a table.

They climbed the stairs slowly, silently. At the top was a long hallway. "This place has more bedrooms than a cheap motel," Joe whispered. "Where do we start?"

"At the beginning," Frank replied. He tried the door to the first room on his right. It was unlocked. He pushed it open and slipped into the room.

Joe was about to follow him when a man suddenly burst out of a doorway down the hall. He was clutching a short, ugly-looking submachine gun, and it was leveled at Joe.

"You're not Vinnie," he growled.

Joe threw his hands up in the air. "I could change my name if it would make you happy," he ventured as he moved away from the door.

"Shut up!" the man snapped. "Who are you? And where's Vinnie?"

Joe started to back slowly toward the stairs. "Come on, I'll show you where he is."

The man moved toward him warily, his eyes riveted on Joe, watching his every move. He didn't notice the partially open door as he passed it. "If you've done anything to Vinnie, I'll—"

He never finished the sentence because Frank had smashed a flowerpot over his head.

Joe whirled around to see his brother standing over the man's limp body, the shattered remains of the pot still clutched in Frank's hands.

He walked down the hall to the door the man had left open. Joe poked his head inside and found Jade's father gagged and tied up in a chair.

"Where's Jade?" Kevin Roberts blurted out as soon as Joe took off the gag. "Is she all right?"

"She's fine," Joe assured him. "She's down on the beach waiting for you."

"Where is everybody?" Frank asked. "We only ran into two of Catlin's goons. There must be more than that."

"Catlin and Gordon left with three or four men about two hours ago," Roberts said. "I think they were going to set up some kind of ambush."

Frank looked at his watch. "For us, I think."

"Gee, I'm sorry we had to spoil all their fun by not showing up," Joe said.

He looked at Jade's father. "What's going on here, anyway? If Thomas Catlin wanted you dead, how come you're still alive? And why are they after Jade? She didn't do anything."

"I didn't understand it myself until this morning," Kevin Roberts said. "That's when Catlin told me about his daughter. She was just a little older than Jade.''

"Was?" Frank said.

"She died in a car accident," Roberts explained, "just before Catlin was released from prison. She was only sixteen."

"So what's that got to do with you and Jade?" Joe asked. "It wasn't your fault."

"Try telling that to Thomas Catlin," Roberts replied grimly. "He thinks that if he hadn't been in jail while she was growing up, his daughter would still be alive."

"And since you put him behind bars," Frank said, "he wants your daughter's life for his."

Kevin Roberts nodded silently.

"We better get out of here," Frank said. "By now they should have figured out we're not playing the game by their rules. They could be back any minute."

They hurried down the stairs to the front hall. Through a window they saw a long, gray limousine barreling down the driveway, followed by the black van.

"Looks like we've got company," Joe observed.

They hustled Kevin Roberts through the dining room and kitchen and out the back door. "You guys go on ahead," Joe said. "There's something I've got to do first."

Frank stopped and turned around. "I'm not going anyplace without you," he said firmly.

"There's no time to argue about it," Joe replied.

"You're right," Frank agreed. He turned to Jade's father and pointed down to the beach. "Jade's waiting down there. Her friends will get you out of here."

"What about you?" Kevin Roberts asked.

"Don't worry," Frank answered. "We know what we're doing." After Roberts left, he turned to his brother. "What are we doing?"

"We've got to buy them some time to escape," Joe said. "We need to set up a diversion."

"Got any ideas?" Frank asked.

Joe grinned. "Ever take a ride in a limo?"

The two brothers sneaked around the side of the house. The limousine and the van had just pulled up in front. The limo driver got out and opened the back door.

A tall, slim man with silver-gray hair emerged. He was dressed casually in white shorts and a shirt. Pete Gordon jumped out of the van just then, and the man barked something at him. Joe couldn't make out the words, but it was clear the man in the white shorts was unhappy about something.

"That must be Catlin," Frank whispered.

"I wish I could see the look on his face when he finds out nobody's home," Joe said.

"I'd rather be a couple miles away," Frank replied.

They waited until Catlin and his men filed into the mansion. Then they dashed over to the empty limousine. The door was unlocked. Frank opened it and was greeted by a loud electronic *beeeeep*. He froze for a second, afraid that he had just set off a car alarm. Then he realized it was only the buzzer to alert the driver that the keys were still in the ignition. He slid behind the wheel and started the engine.

As Joe opened the door on the other side, he heard muffled shouting coming from inside the house. Then he clearly heard Pete Gordon's voice. "The back door's open!" he called out. "I think they headed for the water!"

Joe ran around the limousine and bounded up the stairs to the front door. "Hey!" he shouted. "Somebody's stealing the boss's limo!" Then he dashed back to the limo and jumped in.

Frank hit the gas, and the luxury car tore down the driveway. In the rearview mirror, he could see Gordon come running out the front door—with his gun already drawn. Frank turned the steering wheel left, then right, then left again, swerving the limo from one side of the pavement to the other. He heard a shot ring out, and then another. There was a loud *thunk* as one of the bullets thudded into the trunk of the limo.

Frank kept the gas pedal all the way down, and they sped out of range.

Up ahead loomed the iron gate. It was closed.

"Oops," Joe said. "I think we forgot one minor detail."

"What's this 'we' business?" Frank replied. "This was *your* plan, remember?" He spotted a small remote control unit—like the garage door opener he had turned into a homing device—stuck to the dashboard by a strip of Velcro. He grabbed it, pointed it at the gate, and pushed the button.

The gate began to swing open slowly. But it ground to a halt at about the halfway point. Frank punched the button again. Nothing. The opening was too narrow for the wide limousine.

They were trapped.

Chapter

16

"WHAT'S WRONG?" Joe asked. He could tell there wasn't enough room for the limo to get through the gate. "Why did it stop? Why won't it open?"

"They must have cut the power back at the house!"

"Then I guess it's time for plan B," Joe said.

"Plan B? What's plan B?"

Joe jammed his left foot down on his brother's right foot, pushing the gas pedal to the floor. "Go for it!" he yelled.

The car rocketed forward and smashed into the gate. The iron bars held, but the bolts sunk into the brick wall didn't. The force of the collision snapped rusty old bolts and ripped others out of the brick mortar. The gate crashed to the ground, and the limousine rolled over it and out onto the road.

"Great driving," Joe said, grinning wildly. "Reminds me of the first time we borrowed Dad's car. Remember?"

Frank shot him a look. "Yeah." He glanced in the rearview mirror. "Uh-oh, we've got company."

Joe twisted around to peer out the back window. The black van was closing in from behind. "Think we can lose him somehow?" he asked.

"Not on this road," Frank answered. "Too many twists and turns, and this limo is too long and wide. It doesn't have any maneuverability."

"Plenty of horsepower, though," Joe remarked. "Nice comfy seats, too." He glanced over at his brother. "I bet you could crank her wide open on the highway—and still have a real smooth ride."

"Let's find out," Frank said. He turned onto the Pali Highway, heading back toward Honolulu, the black van following. Frank punched the gas pedal. The limo shot ahead, widening the gap between them and the van.

Joe was right—it had a *very* powerful engine. Frank realized that Catlin probably had had it modified. He checked out the rear window again. The van couldn't keep up. It was dwindling in the distance.

Frank knew that the road would continue to climb upward until after they passed the Nuuanu

Pali. He breathed a little easier as the van grew steadily smaller in the mirror.

Suddenly the engine began to cough. The limo lurched and hesitated, then lurched again. Their speed started to drop. What was wrong?

Frank looked at the control panel. He smacked the steering wheel with his fist and swore silently to himself. "You're not going to believe this," he said. "We're out of gas."

Joe pointed out the window. "There's a turnoff up ahead. If we're lucky, Gordon won't realize we got off the highway until we're long gone."

"Long gone where?" Frank replied. "Off a thousand-foot cliff? That's the turnoff for Nuuanu Pali!"

"Okay, so it's not the greatest choice," Joe admitted. "But it's the only one we've got."

"And if Gordon finds us?" Frank persisted.

Joe shrugged. "I don't know—grow wings and fly away?"

"Terrific," Frank muttered, but he knew his brother was right. They didn't have any choice.

They barely made it to the scenic overlook before the engine sputtered and died. They weren't alone. There was a minivan parked near the concrete observation platform. Two guys were busy taking something out of the back of the van and assembling it on the platform.

"What is that?" Joe asked.

Frank studied the metal tubes and wires. He couldn't make out what it was until one of the guys unfolded a wide and roughly triangular sheet of brightly colored material. The colors reminded him of the para-sail that had snatched Joe and Jade off Maui. But the shape told him it was something else.

"You wanted wings," he said. "There they are."

Frank and Joe hurried over to the platform. One of the guys working on the contraption looked as if he was at least thirty-five years old, but in good shape. The other one was just a kid, not much older than twelve or thirteen.

Frank realized they must be father and son. "Nice hang glider you've got there," he said. "Interesting design, too. Looks like a two-man model."

The older man looked up from his work. "That's right," he said. "That's what happens when you refuse to grow old gracefully around your kids. Pretty soon, they want to play with all your toys."

A stiff wind whipped around them. The sail flapped wildly, and the man struggled to keep the hang glider on the ground.

"Let me help you with that," Frank offered. "Joe, go around and grab the other side."

"Thanks," the man said. "There's a good wind today. We could stay up for hours—sail all the way to Waikiki if we wanted."

"I sure hope so," Joe muttered under his breath.

"Dad!" the boy called from the back of the minivan. "I think we're going to have to repack the parachute."

"Parachute?" Joe asked.

"I've never needed it yet," the man said, "but why take chances?"

"I agree one hundred percent," Frank replied. "Go help your son. We'll take care of the hang glider."

"Thanks again," the man said. "This should only take a couple of minutes."

"Take your time," Joe said. "We're not going anywhere."

The man walked back to join his son. They had their backs to the Hardys, absorbed in the job of refolding the emergency parachute.

Frank quickly checked the hang glider's rigging. "She's ready to go," he told his brother. "Are you?"

Joe shrugged. "Why not? Sometimes you just have to take a chance."

Frank smiled. "I agree one hundred percent."

Joe held the sail steady while Frank slipped into one of the two harnesses. He glanced back over his shoulder. The father and son team hadn't noticed anything yet. But beyond them Joe saw something else—a black van was pulling into the small parking lot.

He ducked under the sail. Frank was still making a few final adjustments to the harness. A large triangular frame made of metal tubing hung down from the crossbar that supported the sail. Joe knew this framework controlled the flight of the hang glider. Suspended in the harness, the pilot made the giant kite go up and down by pushing and pulling the horizontal bar at the base of this control frame.

Joe grabbed the control bar and started running, pulling Frank along in the harness.

"What are you doing?" Frank yelled. "You've got to put on your harness first!"

Joe snagged one arm through the harness. "Hope this is good enough—because here we go!"

The hang glider sailed over the edge of the cliff, but then it nosed down sharply. Joe had one hand hooked in the harness while he clutched desperately at the control bar with the other.

"Let go of the bar!" Frank shouted at him. "You're putting us into a dive!"

Joe took his hand off the control bar and clutched at the harness. Frank shoved the bar forward, and the hang glider leveled out. They caught an updraft and started to climb.

Joe looked back and saw Pete Gordon standing on the observation platform, shaking his fist at the sky.

"Remind me never to complain about airplane seats again," Joe said as he tried to squirm into the harness. It wasn't an easy task. Every time he shifted his weight, the hang glider would pitch to one side. He could see that Frank was constantly fighting the control bar to keep their flight steady.

As they sailed along, Joe thought they probably could have made it all the way to Waikiki if they hadn't gotten off to such a shaky start. But they lost too much altitude while he struggled into position. Now they were too low to catch any more updrafts, and they were gliding steadily downward.

The carpet of trees below them gradually started to break up with the intrusion of occasional houses. "We're going to have to put her down soon," Frank said. "Look for a good clearing."

Joe pointed down. "How about that big lawn over there?"

They were getting dangerously close to the treetops. "It'll have to do," Frank said grimly.

They just managed to clear the trees at the edge of the yard. Ahead there was a sprawling ranch house. And between them and the house was a large swimming pool. They touched down on the grass. But their momentum dragged them forward—right into the shallow end of the pool.

As they splashed around and untangled themselves from the hang glider, Joe looked over at Frank and said, "At least we wore the right clothes."

Frank laughed. They were still wearing the swim trunks they had borrowed from Al Kealoha. "Let's just hope whoever lives here will let a couple of pool-hoppers use the phone. We've got to make a phone call.''

Joe nodded. "And unless these folks want a slightly used and very wet hang glider, maybe they can help us get it back to its owners.''

Two hours later they were back in the hotel suite, dressed in their own clothes. Their father was there, and so were Jade and Kevin Roberts.

"As soon as you called and told me you were all safe and gave me the location of Catlin's headquarters," Fenton said, "I called the police and the FBI. A combined task force hit the place. They nabbed Catlin and four of his men just as they were trying to make their escape.''

"Does that mean we're safe now?" Jade asked.

"It looks that way. Catlin will be behind bars for years," Fenton replied.

Jade looked at her father. "Then can I surf in the Banzai Pipeline competition tomorrow?"

"After what you've been through," Kevin Roberts answered, "how could I say no?"

"What about Pete Gordon?" Frank asked. "Did they catch him yet?"

Fenton shook his head. "No, but it's only a matter of time.''

The next day Frank and Joe drove up to the north shore with Jade to watch her in the competition. The beach was jammed with spectators, reporters, and surfers. Some of them spotted Jade and rushed over to her.

Joe took her surfboard out of the back of the jeep. "Looks like you'll be busy signing autographs and giving interviews," he said. "I'll carry this for you."

They walked down to the beach and people crowded in around them. Frank found himself swept up in a small human wave. He got separated from Joe and Jade and tried to work his way back.

He caught a glimpse of Joe farther up the beach, holding Jade's surfboard over his head. Even though Frank couldn't see Jade through the crowd, he figured she was probably right next to Joe.

Then Frank saw someone else he recognized—a man with a scar over his left eye. He also saw the blue-gray glint of metal in the man's hand.

"Joe!" he screamed. "Jade! Get down!"

It was too late. Pete Gordon had already pushed his way through the crowd—and his gun was leveled right at Jade Roberts.

Chapter

17

At the sound of his brother's voice, Joe whirled around and spotted Gordon.

"He's got a gun!" someone screamed. The crowd backed away from the renegade FBI agent, leaving him a clear shot at both Joe and Jade.

"I should have killed you back at Diamond Head," Gordon said.

Joe glared at him. "You should have *tried*," he growled.

He hurled the surfboard at Gordon. It slammed into his chest, knocking him over. Joe's foot stomped down on the agent's hand, grinding the gun into the sand. Then he was on top of Gordon, pinning him down.

"Had enough yet?" Joe screamed. "Your boss

is already in jail! It's over! You're just too stupid to figure it out!''

Frank shoved through the crowd. He scooped up Gordon's gun and pulled Joe off the hired killer.

Gordon struggled to a sitting position. "You're the one who hasn't figured it out yet. Prison never stopped Thomas Catlin from getting what he wants. He still calls the shots even from behind bars. Lots of guys took one-way rides while Catlin was locked up before. This isn't the end of it. It won't be over until—"

"Until I'm dead," Jade cut in.

Joe turned to her. "I told you I wouldn't let anything happen to you, and I always keep my word."

She smiled weakly. "What can you do, Joe? Hover over me twenty-four hours a day for the rest of my life? They'd just kill you, too. I can't let that happen."

Frank looked down at Pete Gordon. The man was a sleaze and a traitor. He had sold his FBI badge to a gangster. He would go to jail, but for how long? Not long enough, Frank thought. He might even finish off this job when he got out—if Jade survived that long.

He knew Gordon was right. Catlin's goons would keep coming until Jade was dead. That gave him an idea and he stared at his brother. "I guess we'll just have to let Gordon finish the job now."

"Say *what?*" Joe replied in disbelief.

Frank turned to the FBI agent. "What do you suppose would happen if Catlin found out you botched the job and then rolled over on him to save your own skin?"

The look on Gordon's face brought a smile to Frank's lips. "That's what I thought."

"It seems like we just got here yesterday," Frank said as they walked through the Honolulu airport. "I don't know if I'm ready to go home yet—I never even got a chance to work on my tan."

Fenton Hardy stopped at the departure gate and put down his suitcase. "At least the last few days have been uneventful," he replied. "And Thomas Catlin won't be getting much sun for a long time."

"Neither will Pete Gordon," Frank added.

"Pete Gordon won't be getting much *sleep* for a long time, either," Fenton said.

Joe was pacing the floor. "Do you really think it'll work?" he asked his brother. "Do you think Catlin will buy the story that Gordon killed Jade?"

"He only has to believe it long enough for Jade and her father to disappear," Frank reminded him. "When Catlin finds out the truth, Gordon's life in prison is going to be pretty miserable."

Frank put his hand on his brother's shoulder.

"Jade will be safe from now on," he assured him. "Relax."

Joe stopped pacing. "I guess you're right, but I'll never get to see her again."

Frank smiled. "Oh, you never know who you'll run into."

Joe looked over his shoulder to see what his brother was smiling about. He saw a familiar face across the concourse. He walked over slowly and whispered her name. "Jade?"

She smiled softly and shook her head. "Not anymore. Jade's gone—I've got a new name now."

"Where will you and your father go now?" Joe asked.

"It's best if you don't know," she said. "I shouldn't even be here. I don't know if we'll ever really be safe."

Joe reached out and took her hand. "It's over. They won't find you again."

"How can you be sure?" she asked. "They found us once—and that was after fifteen years."

"That was just dumb luck," Joe said. "If Catlin hadn't expanded his operation to Hawaii and gotten involved in illegal gambling on surfing events, they never would have noticed you."

"I guess Nick Hawk didn't help the situation much either," she added.

Joe nodded. "That's right. He didn't know it—but all his betting on Connie focused a lot of attention on *you*. Catlin got greedy. He thought he could make even more money off surfing if he fixed the competition by taking you out of it. It was only later that he realized who you were."

"He saw the picture of me and my father in the surfing magazine," Jade said.

"Right," Joe said. "His goons were carrying around copies of it to identify you."

"Flight four-forty-four for New York now boarding at gate seventeen," a voice announced over the PA system.

Joe glanced over at the boarding area. Frank tapped his watch and pointed at the gate.

"That's my flight," he said. "I have to go."

"I guess this is goodbye, then," she said.

"I guess so," Joe said, but he didn't move.

She looked up into his eyes. "Jade asked me to give you something before you go."

"You don't have to give me anyth—" Joe started to say.

She leaned over and kissed him tenderly. "I'll never forget you, Joe Hardy," she whispered. There was the glimmer of a tear in her eye.

Then she turned and walked away, fading into the crowded airport.

Joe just stood in the middle of the corridor after she was gone.

Frank came up to his brother and waved his hand in front of his face. "Are you okay?" he asked.

Joe flashed his best smile. "Sure. She's a nice

girl, but it never would have worked out between us."

Frank arched his eyebrows. "Oh? You seemed to get along pretty well."

"Get real," Joe replied. "She's a surfer."

"So?"

"So the surfing is *lousy* in Bayport."

Frank and Joe's next case:

The highway can be a very dangerous place—
especially when you're carrying a heavy cargo.
The Hardys have gone undercover, determined
to crack a truck hijacking scheme, but a ruth-
less gang of thugs are just as determined to
run them off the road.

The hijackers are spreading terror on the inter-
states, and whoever gets in their way could end
up on a one-way dead-end street. Someone's
going to eat asphalt, but Frank and Joe are
prepared. They're gunning the engines and riding
the roads on eighteen wheels of diesel-powered
chrome and steel . . . in *Highway Robbery*,
Case #41 in The Hardy Boys Casefiles™.